CONNECTED

Book 1 of the Naquant Traveller series

Deborah Nock

MWA

Cover layout by Nathan Pretlove,
Winter Hill Design, Telford, UK

To John and Adam

You light up my life every single day

ACKNOWLEDGEMENTS

I have wanted to write a book for a very long time, but always found an excuse not to do it. Then I started reading the books by RR Haywood, which introduced me to the idea of really good, self-published stories.

Yet pure laziness stopped me from actually doing anything about it. It took the likes of Ricky Fleet, Suzanne Sussex, Matt Hay, Freedom Matthews, Claire Mulderrig, Markoff Chaney and D.O. Thomas to prove to me that writing a book can be done, and done well, even when you have a very busy life. Even so, this book would simply not exist without the wonderful Angela Smith. She brought together a group of like-minded people, who now form The End of the World Pub – I am proud to call you all my friends.

Thanks to Marc Moore, Matt Hay and Simon Philip for initial encouragement at the early stages, and to Emily from Fantasy Name Generators – a very useful website when you're stuck for inspiration. My heartfelt gratitude goes to my first young readers: Theo and Jamie for reading and enjoying the first incarnation and giving me hope, but also Rose, Sophie and Thomas who were kind enough to try but discovered that the story wasn't for them. Xanthe Seager and Nathan Pretlove also read the first version and provided much-needed guidance and support.

Thanks to Lisa Mann, whose superb and valuable advice regarding the storyline and flow completely changed the book and its audience. Her creativity always amazes me. And to John Wilson and Angela Smith (again) for taking the time to read the final book and make valuable contributions.

Finally, thanks to my mom, Sharon Nock, my sister, Lisa Barratt, and my lovely friend, Victoria Bowen, for being kind enough to read this, despite it being a story that they'd never normally choose. They gave me the confidence to carry on when they told me they enjoyed it anyway. And to Dad, of course, for always being there.

CONTENTS

SO IT BEGINS

'Realize that everything connects to everything else.'

—*Leonardo da Vinci*

Ellen raced down the corridor, wiping sweat out of her eyes into dark curly hair. Gasping desperately into the sterile air of the hospital mortuary, she frantically tried the final room. Knowing this was her last chance, she cried out as the door opened and she half fell inside. Locking it behind her, she grabbed the phone on the large desk and dialled home.

'Yes, can I help you?' asked a soft, rich voice.

Closing her eyes, she could almost see Aaron leaning back in his office chair, long legs sprawling, and her heart tightened.

'Aaron, it's me. Agathe is almost here, I don't have much time. You have to take Evie and go, make sure she's safe. Take Liam's things with you, Agathe mustn't find them.'

'Ellen, no! I'm on my way now, I can stop her, I know I can.'

'Stay where you are,' she ordered. 'You know what you have to do, she'll stop at nothing. She's going to take me like she took all the others. You must protect Evie. You're all she has now, please don't leave my little girl alone.'

She flinched at the pain in his voice as he reluctantly agreed. 'I love you Aaron, never forget,' she whispered, tears streaming down her face. 'Take care of my beloved Evie.'

Gently she replaced the receiver before she could change her mind, cutting him off in mid-sentence. Breathing deeply, trying to calm herself, she sat in the leather swivel chair and waited.

It wasn't long before she heard loud footsteps echoing down the corridor. Her pulse quickened, and she rested her feet on the desk in a show of indifference. Even though she knew it would come, the crash of the door startled her as it was kicked open. She crossed her arms to hide her shaking hands.

'Well, you've found me. What do you want?' she demanded as a hulking figure entered the room. 'I hope you've got a very good excuse for damaging that door, Emil. My boss won't be too pleased.'

He smiled at her mockingly, then deferentially stepped aside to let a small, matronly woman enter.

'Ellen!' she scolded, walking calmly to the desk. 'What *is* all this fuss about? We only want to talk to you. No need for this nonsense. Come to OPOL headquarters, you can see for yourself how you *will* help me.'

'Ha!' scoffed Ellen. 'Your little old lady act doesn't fool

me. I know you too well, remember. And especially him,' she said, glancing at Emil in contempt. 'I'm not going anywhere.'

The woman's pale blue eyes narrowed as she watched her. Her lips tightened and she turned to Emil. 'We'll have to do this the hard way, my dear. I'm sure you have no objections. Get her.'

Impassively, the big man pounced towards Ellen. Anticipating him, she grabbed the nearest object and hurled it.

'You haven't changed, you're still nothing but a vicious bully!' she shouted.

He barely registered as the heavy phone bounced off his muscular chest, instead reaching over the desk to grab her by her shoulders. His fingers dug in and she squealed in pain as he lifted her out of the chair, dragging her towards him. She scraped her nails down his arms, trying to loosen his powerful grip, but he simply laughed as he set her on her feet and pinned her arms behind her. Ellen opened her mouth to scream for help.

'Don't bother, girl,' said the older woman. 'Nobody can hear you down here. You should know that, you've worked here long enough. What a waste of talent, you could have been one of my top agents instead of poking around in dead bodies in this cold, lifeless place.'

'I would never work for you again, I'm not one of your minions like him,' she said, still trying to break free from Emil's strong grasp. 'You're cruel, ruthless and lacking in any morals whatsoever. OPOL used to be good until you got your grubby hands on it. Now your agents do nothing but seize control. You make me sick.'

She stopped and glared at Agathe. 'There is nothing you can do to make me work for OPOL again, not while you're in charge.'

Agathe laughed, a brittle tinkling sound that made Ellen grit her teeth.

'I don't want you as one of my agents *now*, dear Ellen. It's far too late for that. Besides, you have something that belongs to me. No, you're much more useful to me in other ways. I don't want to spoil the surprise though. Emil, hold her tight while I contact lifoNET. No need to be gentle.'

Ellen whimpered as Emil crushed her tightly against his chest. A familiar wave of dizziness made her head spin as Agathe adjusted her el-VA and opened a path for them.

'Evie…,' sobbed Ellen, her heart breaking.

The web of quantum filaments unfolded before them, their magnificent beauty unable to touch her desolation. She sagged in Emil's arms, defeated, as lifoNET propelled their minds along a single, glowing strand, and their atoms dispersed into an indistinct nebulous mass.

As ever, she didn't register the transfer. She'd realised a long time ago that their consciousness wasn't strong enough to cope with the magnitude of the Quantum Universal Network – better known as the net – and not remembering was a safeguard. Slowly, awareness began to return as lifoNET finished the incredibly complex calculations that would imprint their quantum state onto new atoms at OPOL headquarters.

Immediately she began to struggle, hoping to escape while Emil was weakened. But like her he was a seasoned teleporter, and he squeezed her closer. Using one big hand to restrain her, he used the other to pull out his neural disruptor. Pointing it at her head, he gestured for her to follow Agathe who was walking towards a solid metal door. As the older woman approached, she keyed in a code, allowed the computer system to scan her retinas and fingerprints, then spat into a small tube that appeared from the console.

'Tight security,' said Agathe, noting Ellen's disgust. 'The system analyses my DNA as well, and saliva is one of best ways of obtaining it. Nobody can enter here unless I am present.'

With a smooth hiss, the door slid open to reveal a vast room filled with an enormous, intricate machine. The central column towered above their heads, surrounded by many clusters of large capsules that hummed gently in harmony. A bank of handheld devices covered one wall, with many empty slots.

'lifoNET,' declared Agathe proudly, sweeping her arm towards the array of serenely pulsating lights. 'My life's greatest achievement. A supercomputer with unparalleled processing power and sophisticated artificial intelligence. Accessed using a lifoNET Virtual Assistant, or el-VA as my agents call it. The only way of travelling the net, if you're not a naquant like yourself, Ellen.'

Ellen sneered at her dismissively. 'I have seen it before, you know. The greatest invention ever, wasted to satisfy your lust for power.'

Agathe smiled coldly. 'You can't goad me, child. You are nothing, you have no idea what true control is. I have spent my life doing things that some might regard as…bad…using people who would eat *you* alive, and now I am reaping the rewards.'

Shivering at the ruthlessness in her voice, Ellen asked, 'Why have you been monitoring me, why did you send Aaron to watch over me?'

'He is one of our best agents, devoted to our cause. At least I thought he was. Clearly you have corrupted him. He will pay for his betrayal.'

She paused, eyes flinty, then continued. 'I needed to know where all the naquants were. When we found you again, I sent him to make sure you didn't disappear into the net.'

'You must have known that I would never leave Evie alone like that?'

'I couldn't be sure, not all of us are so maternal. But Aaron told me you were soft-hearted, and he was right. You should have escaped while you had the chance. I need your talents and I will have them.'

Agathe looked at her hungrily. 'lifoNET needs power, enormous reserves of power. But not just electricity. It needs enough quantum energy to teleport us across the net, and there is only one way to get that.'

She strolled over to one of the capsules and gestured for Ellen to look closer. Emil dragged her over to the transparent cover. Reaching on her toes, she squinted as she tried to glimpse what was lurking beneath the milky liquid. With a scream, she fell back into Emil's arms and buried her head into his chest. Almost involuntarily he reached up to comfort her, before letting his arm fall back as Agathe coolly regarded him.

'Liam…' whispered Ellen, the wrinkled, emaciated face of Evie's father seared into her mind. 'What have you done do to him? What have you done?' she screeched, ripping free of Emil and launching herself towards Agathe. With an agonised cry, she stopped as Emil grabbed her hair and yanked her backwards.

Sobbing, she asked, 'I thought he was dead, why is he in there?'

'I'm using his naquant power, of course. All the capsules contain a naquant, that is the only way that lifoNET will work properly. Why do you think I have been chasing you for so long? I need you to power lifoNET.'

Ellen paled and stared in revulsion at the clusters, knowing that each must contain one of her friends. The rumour was that those who had disappeared had teleported to a distant world and chosen not to come back. Now she knew the terrible truth.

'But why now, why have you captured me now?'

'Two reasons. First, come closer and take a good look at

Liam. He doesn't have much power left. One more trip and he'll be empty, a husk, no use to me. I need a replacement, it's as simple as that. And I know you have great power, much more than Liam ever did. You'll be perfect.'

Ellen stared at her in horror, unable to look again at what remained of her husband. 'You wouldn't do that, please, no. There must be some other way to power lifoNET?'

'No, no other way. No easier way, anyway. But I might be merciful, if you do something for me. You scratch my back, I'll scratch yours. You know how it works.'

Ellen looked at her, her heart sinking. She knew where this was heading.

'Give me the plans, Ellen. Liam stole from me, he hid what is mine, and now he is being punished. You might avoid all that if you tell me where he put my plans. If you don't, you will never see your daughter again.'

Ellen bit her lip, uncertain. Then sighed, resigned.

'I will never tell you anything Agathe. Those plans will tell us how to destroy lifoNET. You will never get your hands on them.'

'Oh, I wouldn't be so sure. I was certain you wouldn't tell me anything, I know how sickeningly brave you are. Well, not to worry, I'll get them soon enough. Emil, prepare her.'

Ellen lashed out as Emil lifted her off her feet and carried her to a capsule that had begun to open. She struggled frantically, trying to find a way to break free as he lay her down and kept her pinioned while he secured her limbs and hooked her up to the machine. His fingers trembled slightly as he tightened the restraints.

'And don't worry about Evie,' chuckled Agathe. 'I'll be keeping a very close eye on her. I'll soon have an empty capsule to fill after all. With two naquants as parents, she will surely have the same talents. And her youth means she will last a lot longer than you will. I have no doubt you've left the plans with her, so I think I'll get Emil to bring her in now, *educate* her about her new life. What fun we'll have. Think about that while you're in the capsule, Ellen. If you're able to think at all, of course. Goodbye, my dear.'

She laughed, delighted, and sauntered out of the room.

Ellen's desolate, grief-stricken cries echoed in the vast room as Emil attached the last of the tubes and monitors and closed the capsule door. As it filled with the cloudy liquid, she felt herself drift. Her final sight was of the lingering, wistful look he gave her, before his face hardened and he turned to follow Agathe. Ellen's mind shut down, and the energy began to flow.

.

1. A TASTY MORSEL

'Tell me what you eat, and I will tell you what you are.'

—Anthelme Brillat-Savarin

E vie woke with a start, sweat trickling down her back, and wept as the terror of the nightmare lingered. She had been dreaming about her mother for the past month, and the dreams were getting stronger. Almost as soon as she was asleep, she would become convinced that her mother was trapped in a dark, lonely place, screams absorbed by the soft confines of her cell. Evie would run along a broken path towards her, sharp stones tearing her bare feet, the landscape surrounding her foggy and indistinct, lit by the occasional vivid blue streak. Her heart would be pounding and breath running short, but no matter how fast she ran, she could never reach her.

Angrily, she wiped the tears from her eyes. Her mom was dead, Aaron had told her so. Ellen had gone to work at the mortuary one morning, and had simply disappeared, not even a body left to bury. Evie vividly remembered that terrible day. Aaron had picked her up from school, the car piled high with bags.

'We have to leave, now. Our lives are in danger. Your mother…' he had stopped, his voice cracking with grief. 'They killed her, Evie. I wanted to rescue her, but you were all she cared about.' He bowed his head, overcome, then quickly bundled her into the car. 'She wanted you to be safe, so we must go.'

Evie had curled onto the back seat and cried hot, angry tears, her heart cracking with sorrow. It had taken her a long time to readjust to life, comforted by Aaron in his kind, bumbling way. He would never tell her who was after them though. 'When you're old enough, I'll tell you everything,' was his only response.

Now the nightmares had begun, and Evie couldn't shake the feeling that her mother was alive somewhere, unable to escape. And the intense dreams seemed to be leaking into everyday life. Staring at the whitewashed ceiling above her bed sometimes made it dissolve, the space around her expanding into an enormous web of pulsating nodes linked by shimmering strands. Each time, she had seen a single node sputtering madly and felt it *pull* her towards it. She wasn't sure what terrified her most – the thought of losing her mind, or what would happen if she let go of reality and followed that thread. She hadn't yet found the courage to do so.

She put her head in her hands and gently tugged the dark

wisps of hair entwined around her fingers. Worrying about hallucinations wasn't going to solve anything. It was time to go out, and she really needed a shower. She locked herself in the bathroom, switched on the water, and stepped into the cascade of water. As she watched the silvery streaks gush down, stray droplets dancing in the steamy air, the now familiar sensation overwhelmed her as the complexity of the web unfolded, leaving her weak and dazed. Seeing the flickering node that had been calling her for weeks, and overcome by an insatiable desire to know what would happen, she *willed* herself along the rhythmic pulse, losing consciousness as she did.

She opened her eyes to find herself sliding rapidly down a smooth slope towards a floor littered with razor-sharp rocks. Screaming, she tried desperately to hold on but couldn't grip the glassy substance. Heart racing, she forced herself to look down from the dizzying heights to find a soft landing. Directly below, she spotted a dark fuzzy mass, so she steeled herself and jumped, landing on the spongy mound.

Sinking her shaking hands into the blue, velvety substance, she closed her eyes, blew her dark fringe from her face, and tried to get her breathing under control. A worrying thought crossed her mind and she looked down quickly, sighing in relief when she realised she was wearing clothes.

Deciding to climb down the rest of the way, she sat up and turned around. Then scooted back with a squeal as two eyes swivelled to watch her. Quickly realising she must be on the back of some creature, she tried to scrabble over the edge but was caught dangling in the grasps of a huge, hairy pincer.

'Be still,' commanded a deep, yet piercing voice. 'How did you escape?'

Shocked, Evie stopped squirming as the words echoed around her brain without first reaching her ears.

'No matter, I've got you now,' continued the voice. With a quick flick of two of its many legs, it wrapped Evie up in a sticky substance, dangled her underneath its body, and scuttled up the same slope from which Evie had just fallen.

As they climbed higher and higher, the wind stripping tears from her eyes, Evie could see strange, dome-like dwellings balanced precariously on tall, narrow supports. Linking them together was a web of thin threads that shivered in the strong gusts. Scurrying across the web, making her skin crawl, were giant, spider-like creatures with long, bristly legs and bloated, bulbous bodies.

Evie whimpered as she realised why she might be trussed up like a fly. She had learned about spiders at school, but they didn't fascinate her quite so much now that *she* might be next on the menu. In a frenzied panic, she tried to free herself. But the bindings were too tight and too sticky, and she was too far above ground. So she tried to relax, chaotic thoughts swirling, and waited to see how things would develop.

She swung beneath the body of the beast, distracted from her fear by a gentle fragrance in the breeze. A fresh yet heady scent that reminded her of warm afternoons in grassy meadows. Even from this height, she could see great flowers dotting the landscape, a kaleidoscope of colour and shape, with large fleshy petals that draped lazily across a bed of broad white leaves. But many of the flowers were pale and sickly, the leaves mottled black and curling at the edges, blemishing the view. Briefly, Evie wondered what was causing the disease, but the thought was swept away as the creature anchored itself to one of the threads between the domes and swung across. The wind and swift motion tore Evie's breath away and she passed out.

When she came to, she was no longer bound. Rubbing at her face to clear her head, she sat up to take in her surroundings. She was being held in a cavernous dome, trapped inside a huge cage. Her eyes grew wide as she watched hundreds of the giant spiders scurrying and jumping everywhere, over the floor, the walls and ceilings, and even over each other. A quiet moan escaped her lips at the scraping of tiny claws, the rustling of hairy legs, and the clacking of chitinous mandibles. Stiff with fear, she tried to see a way of escaping.

As she looked around, she noticed many creatures had deformed limbs and weeping sores that marred their iridescent patches. Moving cautiously towards the barrier to get a closer look, the hem of her t-shirt brushed the glistening bars and stuck fast. She tugged to free it, lightly at first, then with increasing force. With a final ferocious tug, the fabric tore loose and she fell into a heap onto a floor covered in dry, grey fragments. She scrabbled backwards to avoid any further contact, and bumped into someone standing right behind her.

'Oh, sorry,' she exclaimed, climbing hastily to her feet. 'I didn't…see you,' she said slowly, tipping her head back to look at the long, gangly figure towering over her. Standing around seven feet tall, with a triangular head and large bulbous eyes, the humanoid leapt into the air at the sound of her voice, carefully avoiding the sticky bars overhead. The sunlight streaming through the wide windows shone through its gossamer wings as it gracefully landed a fair distance away from her. Mouth gaping in astonishment, Evie turned her head to see several others all staring at her in much the same way.

'There is no need to screech,' admonished the first one, tipping his head to one side as though to clear it. 'I can hear your thoughts quite well. You are obviously not one of our younglings, even though you have no wings. My name is Lepos. What are you, and where are you from?'

Evie clutched her head, as the voice resonated through it. 'Don't do that,' she pleaded. 'It makes my brain itch.'

'This *is* how civilised beings communicate,' he said gently, clearly trying not to cause her any more discomfort. 'We haven't used our voices for many generations. We would appreciate it if you would do the same, as it is most painful.'

'Sor…,' began Evie out loud, before trying again with only her mind. 'Sorry. You're the first telepaths I've ever met. I'm a human, my name is Evie. I…I'm not entirely sure how

I got here. I followed the web and it brought me here. But I have no idea why, and even less idea how to get back.'

The other captives looked at each other in alarm. 'Are you an agent of the Araneans?' Lepos whispered in her head, gesturing towards the skittering throng.

'No, I only just got here,' Evie said. 'If those spider things are Araneans, who are you?'

'We are the Volatis. It is our sacred duty to care for the Magna plants that cover this world. At least, it was – before the Araneans began eating us.'

Images of terror and death flashed through Evie's mind, swept along by crushing sadness. Evie stifled a sob.

'We have tried to fight back. But they are too strong, and we are not built for war. Even though our elders have wings and can fly very fast when attacked, we need to carry our young ones. And the Araneans are skilled jumpers; they spring high into the air to capture us with their sticky nets, or fire poisonous hairs from their legs. We fly as high as we can to keep out of their way. But we must eat and sleep eventually.'

Lepos hung his head in shame. 'It was how I was captured, along with my family. I was exhausted from constantly being on the run, always hiding in fear. I fell asleep during my watch. And now we are waiting for the Araneans to hold their feast.'

Evie stared wide-eyed at the Volatis. 'You can't let them eat you, there must be some other way! We must get out of this cage. Quick, through the floor, can you dig down?'

She fell to her knees and began scraping away the debris,

mounds of old, blackened scales and dry, transparent fragments.

'Stop!' cried Lepos, pulling Evie to her feet, 'This is where we are thrown after being sucked dry. What you see is all that remains of their bodies.'

Evie gasped and wiped her filthy hands across her jumper in a vain attempt to clean them, her eyes filling with tears.

'I'm so sorry,' she whispered.

Seeing her distress, Lepos stretched out his arms and wings and wrapped them around her. As they stood entwined, a commotion began at the cage door and a terrified scream assaulted Evie's mind. Clapping her hands over her ears, she watched as several enormous Araneans heaved their bulk through the door and began wrapping Volatis like flies.

'Run!' Lepos cried as he was bundled in the sticky mesh. His eyes flicked towards the open door, 'You can't help us now, save yourself.'

Evie took off, aiming for the gap between the two biggest Araneans. Just as she reached the door, a large, hairy leg thumped down and blocked her exit. 'Not so fast, little runner. You'll make a tasty morsel,' mocked the Aranean. She slumped in defeat as it prepared her for dinner.

Evie was dumped unceremoniously onto the floor of a pristine, white chamber. Grimacing in pain, she rolled to her knees, struggling against her sticky restraints.

'Hush,' boomed a voice in Evie's mind. 'You cannot

escape, and I need to eat.'

Evie swivelled her head to see an Aranean standing over the thrashing body of what appeared to be an older Volatis hanging from long threads, its eyes wide in terror. Her mind recoiled from its keening. As she watched open-mouthed, a long, sharp proboscis darted down and into the Volatis, killing it instantly. She retched as the Aranean began greedily slurping the juices from the corpse. Less than a minute later, the old Volatis had been sucked dry and the husk casually discarded, left dangling like some macabre puppet.

'No!' shrieked Evie, unable to help herself. She quickly realised her mistake when the Aranean scuttled towards the sound.

'What *are* you?' it mused, rolling her over and noting her lack of wings. 'You are not of the Volatis, where did you come from?'

'Get off me, you great brute, and I'll tell you,' yelled Evie, squirming under its heavy leg.

Great eyes blinking in surprise, the Aranean released the pressure and Evie struggled to sit up.

'I have not heard a voice since our race was still primitive,' said the Aranean, looking at Evie thoughtfully. 'I will ask you again, where are you from?'

'Not from here, that's for sure,' replied Evie. 'I followed a strand in the web and it led me to you.'

The Aranean stepped back in shock. 'The web…do you mean the network, which connects all living things?'

'I don't know, maybe. I call it the web because that's what

it looks like to me.' Wistfully, she added, 'It's the most beautiful sight.'

'It is indeed, there is nothing more wondrous than the connections between Life. This changes everything. Were you sent by OPOL?'

Evie frowned, wondering what answer would place her in greatest danger. 'I travelled by myself,' she said eventually, evading the question. 'To be honest, this is the first time I've done it and it's pretty terrifying. Especially when people get eaten in front of you!'

'Do not fret, you're safe. For now. I assume you're a naquant who has begun to travel the net.' It began slicing at her bindings. 'Your kind are most revered on our world, and it means I cannot eat you.'

'Yeah, thanks for that…' replied Evie, raising an eyebrow. She bent down to hide her relief, wondering what a naquant was, and rubbed her arms and legs to get the blood flowing again.

Then she put her hands on her hips and demanded, 'Why are you eating the Volatis? It's horrible to eat someone who can talk to you!' She shuddered. 'And to leave the body hanging as though it doesn't matter at all, not even a decent burial. Well, words fail me.'

She glared up into its vast eyes, fear dissolving in the face of this atrocity.

To her astonishment, the Aranean looked away, unable to meet her eyes. 'It is of some sorrow to us, I admit. We were once allies.' It stared back in defiance. 'But we are the dominant race, and we have to eat. Meat makes us big and strong.'

It reared up, front legs waving threateningly, and hissed at her. Evie gulped, but held her ground, scowling.

The Aranean sank back to the floor and sighed. 'We need to feed our young. The Volatis I consume will be regurgitated and fed to my offspring.'

As it spoke, a monkey-sized Aranean appeared from its back and jumped onto Evie's head. Knowing that to do otherwise would be the death of her, she froze as every instinct urged her to tear it away and stamp on it repeatedly. Lifting her arm, amazed at its steadiness, she gently patted the slender but muscular legs caressing her face until it lost interest and returned to the safety of its parent. Evie closed her eyes and shivered, the feel of the creature lingering on her skin and in her mind.

The Aranean looked at her in amusement, sensing her revulsion. 'You are well disciplined, little one. What is your name?'

'Evie,' she replied, 'What's yours?'

'I am Vespera, the eldest Aranean and matriarch. I speak for my people, and for all of Aranea.'

'You do not speak for the Volatis,' cried Lepos, bound and hanging from the ceiling. 'You, who were once our friends, who have hunted and eaten us, who have decimated our planet. You do *not* speak for us.'

'Be quiet, you have no rights here. We were told a long time ago that Araneans were the most powerful race on this planet, but that we needed to grow even bigger and stronger to rule properly. Emil told us that if we didn't start eating meat, we would begin to die out.'

Vespera waved a front leg, agitated. 'We refused to let that happen. The tips of the Magna plants were no longer enough, we needed flesh. I suppose we could have eaten the dolosans, the vermin who shelter within to protect the plants, but they are too ferocious for us to capture. Emil persuaded us that the Volatis would do perfectly well instead, as they are a lesser race. It is regrettable, but it is the way of Life.'

Evie looked at Vespera in astonishment, 'Who is Emil, and why on earth would you listen to him?'

'He is from OPOL, of course. The agency has always known what is best for each society.'

Hmm, best for the Araneans but clearly not the Volatis, Evie thought.

To Vespera, she said, 'Let me get this right. You used to eat the tips from plants, which were being protected by the dolosans. How did you get hold of the tips, if you couldn't reach them?'

'That was our role,' said Lepos, slowly turning as his hungry guard pawed at his captive in anticipation. 'We live off the dolosa larvae and cull the mature adults when they become too numerous. Our wings give us an advantage, they allow us to stay out of reach of their poisonous claws and fangs. They are very fast, but they can't jump. We also transport the Magna seeds so that new plants can grow. We *used* to harvest the tips, so the Araneans could eat them. When the Araneans started to kill and eat us instead, the dolosans got out of control and the plants started to die.'

Evie licked her lips, thinking while she watched Vespera. A small, still voice inside was urging her to question the great beast further.

'When your ancestors first started to evolve,' she asked her slowly, 'were they eating meat?'

'No, I wouldn't have thought so. We had lived off the Magna tips for countless generations.'

'When did your people become diseased? I see some that are clearly unhealthy.'

Vespera looked at her fellow Araneans, many bedraggled and sickly. Her mandibles chittered in concentration. In a low voice, she said, 'The first defects began to appear soon after we started eating the Volatis.'

Evie looked at her, eyebrows raised, the connection obvious in her mind.

'Didn't it ever occur to you that eating your neighbours might not have been a good idea?' she asked, sharply.

Impassive eyes stared at her for a long moment, then Vespera drew herself up to her full, terrifying height and roared. She lurched forward, knocking Evie over and pinning her to the ground.

'What are you saying, child?' she growled menacingly, hot breath blasting Evie's face. 'Are you daring to suggest that we were somehow tricked by Emil? That we Araneans were wrong to assert our rightful dominance? That we shouldn't advance our species by enriching our bodies and minds with the nutrients provided by the Volatis? Do you really think we could be so simple as to be fooled that easily by a mere man? Who are you, you little creature, to contradict the collective wisdom of the Araneans?'

'I'm no-one,' cried Evie, struggling beneath the weight of the legs holding her down. 'I don't know anything much. But I *can* see that your race is likely allergic to one of those nutrients you are praising so much.'

Pushing in vain against the thick hairy leg, she demanded hoarsely, 'Let me sit up so I can talk to you, I can't breathe.'

With a last warning increase in pressure that made Evie gasp, Vespera moved backwards and waited as she rolled over to recover.

'Well, out with it,' she commanded imperiously. 'I'm sure we're all eager to hear what you have to say.'

Evie stood, wincing at the pain in her chest. Gathering her courage, she tried to calm the enraged Aranean.

'I don't think you're simple, far from it. Maybe you and Emil didn't realise that the Volatis might be incompatible with your digestive systems. Whether it is right or wrong to eat them is not my decision to make. But it seems clear to me that eating them is making you sick. You need to change your diet, before you all get so ill that you can't recover.'

'But what can we eat if the Volatis are not suitable? I doubt they will ever agree to harvest the Magna tips for us again.'

Evie looked over at Lepos dangling in his restraints.

'Lepos, could you find it in your heart to help the Araneans?'

'If it means my people will no longer be eaten, then yes. We don't forget easily though,' warned Lepos, glowering at Vespera with undisguised hatred.

'It may be that Emil was telling the truth, of course, perhaps the Araneans really do need to eat meat?' suggested Evie, tentatively. 'Not Volatis flesh though!' she added hastily, hearing Lepos growl in her mind. 'Vespera, would you try the dolosans that the Volatis cull, if they agree to help you?'

Vespera closed her eyes in contemplation, then drew herself up proudly. 'I will consider your suggestion and put it to the clan leaders. I will not promise anything, but maybe we could work together. Not as equals though, you understand,' she added disdainfully.

Once again, Evie felt the anger radiate from Lepos and realised that although her solution seemed simple, it would take generations before the two races could work in harmony once more.

'Guards, cut down these Volatis and set them free,' Vespera ordered, already dismissing them from her mind. 'Quick, jump to it!'

The guards began slicing at the sticky bonds, clearly disappointed that their next meal was walking away alive, making the Volatis tense in anger as they quickly crept away before the Aranean matriarch changed her mind.

'Thank you, youngster,' said Vespera gravely, content that her race might flourish again. 'It seems we may be in your debt.'

'Oh, it was nothing really,' replied Evie, rubbing her nose in embarrassment. 'Sometimes everything is much simpler when you look at a problem through a stranger's eyes. I think you would have worked it out soon enough anyway. Now I just need to find a way home.'

She walked over to the window and leaned against the transparent covering, gazing at the graceful, swooping structures outlined against the soft pink sky. She smiled gently. 'It's a beautiful place, for sure. But Aaron will worry if I don't return soon. Do you know how I can get back, Vespera?'

With a final glance at the landscape, she turned back towards the giant creature – and slammed her head against one of the low tubular beams supporting the chamber. *Ow!* she thought indignantly, as her consciousness was flung back across the network, leaving only disorganised atoms behind.

…CONNECTING…

E vie shook her head, disoriented as the water cascaded around her. Feeling faint, she put her hand against the wall to steady herself, then let her head drop. She knew it, she *was* going mad! She was still in the shower, not on a planet full of giant spider-like creatures. She bit her lip to stop it trembling. It had felt so real, her skin still remembered muscular legs crawling across her body. She shuddered and closed her eyes. An hallucination, that's all it was, brought on by severely disturbed sleep. It would be a padded cell next if she wasn't careful.

She sighed, rubbed her face, and stepped out of the shower, shivering despite the warm air. Wrapped in a thick towel, she rummaged around in her wardrobe, trying to find some decent clean clothes. After a futile search, she realised that Aaron had forgotten to do the washing yet again. Still thinking about Vespera and Lepos, wondering whether they could make a new start, then angrily cursing her overactive imagination, she wandered into Aaron's bedroom. He had often told her how similar she was to Ellen, especially now she was growing up, and she wondered if any of her mom's old clothes would fit her now.

She opened the door of the large fitted wardrobe and gaped at the boxes piled high inside. She hadn't realised he had kept so much that belonged to her mother. Feeling like she was prying, she removed some boxes to see what lay behind. At the very back, stuffed into the corner, was a large suitcase engraved with the initials, EBB – Ellen Bethany Brook. She heaved the case out of the wardrobe and onto the bed, sneezing violently in the clouds of dust.

Flipping open the brass latches, she eased up the lid. A familiar scent of lemon and freesias rose with it, bringing tears to her eyes. Her gaze fell onto the framed photograph lying in the case, and the tears fell. Her father stood smiling, the sun catching his blond curly hair, his arm wrapped tightly around his much shorter wife. The camera had caught Ellen's dark curls mid-bounce as she turned to look up at Liam, a mischievous smile on her face.

Evie gently stroked the glass, storing the half-forgotten faces in her mind. Her father had died when she was only small, but she still remembered strong arms swinging her high into the air, making her shiver with excitement. Loneliness tugged at her as she laid the photograph down and turned to the suitcase once more.

Folded neatly inside were delicate sweaters and soft, worn jeans, beautiful floral dresses, and several of the gorgeous silk scarves that Ellen had loved. Gently holding each item against her and looking in the mirror, Evie realised some might fit. She began to replace those that were clearly too big. As she did, she noticed that the bottom of the case was loose in one corner.

Curious, she worked her fingernail underneath and slowly lifted it to reveal a small package wrapped in another silk scarf. She unravelled it to find three strange objects. The first looked like a metal curtain ring, above which were suspended two smaller rings joined in a column by rods. Within each of the small rings was a lens, one deep blue and the other sea green, while the third was empty. The second item looked like an eyepiece from a telescope, split into three rotating parts. Finally, there was a small disk, with two straight grooves cut into one side and a metal rod protruding from the other. The edge of the disk was engraved with strange markings. Everything was made from a dark grey metal that readily absorbed the weak bedroom light.

Evie picked up the lenses and jumped as a sharp tingle ran through her fingers. Placing them back on the bed, she cautiously touched the other two items and felt her skin prickle once more. The flow of energy reminded her of how she had felt when she had followed the strand to Aranea. She looked more closely and wondered if the objects might fit together if there were more parts. Intrigued, she carefully put everything back in the case, and bundled it into the wardrobe.

Quickly dressing in her mother's clothes, she experienced a strange pang of recognition when she caught sight of her short, wiry frame in the mirror. Wishing desperately that her mom was here to talk to, she decided to go for a walk. Her mind was whirling with recent events and the strange package she had found, and she needed to clear her head. She headed towards the nearby park, lost in thought.

Emil slowly circled the park again, watching for any familiar faces. His large hands were thrust into deep pockets that hid his el-VA, his face partially hidden by a thick scarf, despite the warmth of the early spring day. He had only been waiting a short time, but was already becoming hot and impatient.

They had to be here somewhere, lifoNET was never wrong. He had noticed an unusual disturbance in the net only an hour ago by Earth standards, a surge of energy that had attracted his attention. Normally a small blip like that would have gone unnoticed because there was always intense activity in the network. But he had been monitoring Aranea at the time, a world in which he needed to keep control or face Agathe's wrath.

Investigating more closely, he had seen that the energy spike linked back to Earth and his pulse had quickened. He knew there were no other naquants left on Earth and guessed that Aaron, or maybe even Evie at last, had travelled the net to Aranea. Hurriedly downloading the coordinates, he teleported into the park, relishing the thought of finally catching them.

He had spent the time prowling around, waiting,

watching time crawl by on his el-VA. He was just debating whether to look around the streets when he stopped suddenly, the colour draining from his face as he caught sight of somebody on the nearby path. *Ellen, it can't be! She's trapped in lifoNET, there's no way she could have escaped.* Heart racing, he moved behind a tree so he could watch her without being seen.

Still wrapped in confusion, Evie trudged through the quiet park, head down and lost in thought. As she walked deeper through a grove of trees, enveloped in silence, a small, furtive sound startled her. She stopped, searching the early morning gloom for movement.

Her mouth went dry and her bladder tightened when she saw the tall man lurking in the dark shade of the tree. Her eyes widened when she saw him watching her intently, and she nervously licked her dry lips. Realising that they were alone, she walked faster, anxious to reach the safety of the shops, her heart racing. Heavy footsteps landed on the path behind and she began to run, panicking when the footsteps quickened in time with hers. Gasping in fright, she turned her head and cried out as a long arm stretched towards her, its massive hand about to grab her.

She stumbled and fell backwards. As she did, a short, compact body appeared from the undergrowth and flung itself at the towering figure. Wiry arms gripped the man around his legs, causing him to stagger and fall to one side.

'Run!' shouted the boy, as he struggled with the big man, his silvery hair disappearing under the man's bulk. 'I can't hold him much longer.'

Evie scrambled to her feet but hesitated, torn between helping the boy and escaping.

'Go!' he yelled, 'Get to safety, now.'

With a sob, Evie turned and sprinted out of the park, disappearing into the warren of streets. The tears flowed at the sound of the man cursing loudly and a grunt of pain as the boy was struck backwards into a tree by a heavy blow.

2. DAUGHTERS OF WIND AND BLOOD

'Prepare, prepare the iron helm of war…Soldiers, prepare! Be worthy of our cause.'

—William Blake

'There is no instance of a nation benefitting from prolonged warfare.'

—Sun Tzu, The Art of War

In the days that followed, Evie had been unable to forget sound of the boy's distress, another element that wove itself into her already haunted dreams. A few hours after the incident, wracked with guilt and curiosity, she had cautiously returned to the park to see if she could find him. But there were no signs that he or the strange man had ever been there.

Despite her fears, she decided not to worry Aaron by mentioning it. The nightmares were getting worse and once or twice she had caught him watching her, concerned by the dark shadows staining her pale face. She knew she would have to talk to him sooner or later. In the meantime, thankful for the school holidays, she rarely ventured outside, terrified at the thought of being followed again. But she found no respite at home, with the relentless fear that she was losing her grip on reality.

The second time she travelled, there was no warning. One moment she was sitting in the armchair, half reading, half drowsing. The next, she was twisting and tumbling through the air. Terrified screams ripped from her throat as the wind buffeted her body. She thrashed wildly, certain she was going to die, then flattened herself and stretched out her arms in a desperate attempt to slow her descent. She yelled in astonishment as thick, membranous material joining her arms and legs opened in response and she shot high into the sky.

Almost immediately, the roaring of the wind abated, giving her chance to breathe. Wobbling uncertainly as she glided through the air, the adrenalin surged through her and shivers ran along her body. She was utterly terrified but also exultant as she lifted one arm and her body turned like a plane. Lifting the other, she shouted in glee as she swooped through the air. But whoops of joy quickly turned to terror as she approached the flat top of a mountain. Realising she had no idea how to land, she aimed towards a grassy slope, curled into a ball, and braced herself for the undoubtedly painful impact.

She woke up in the cold, wet grass, surrounded by a sea of curious young faces.

'I found her like this,' piped a voice, prodding her with something sharp. 'I only went into the armoury to fetch my sword for practice. When I came back, there she was.'

'Don't do that Mia, haven't you learned anything from training! Never use the point unless you mean to kill. Honestly, you youngsters.'

A heart-shaped face surrounded by a halo of golden curls peered closely at Evie. 'I think she's waking up! Quick, stand back and give her some room. And weapons ready – she isn't one of ours, she must have sneaked in to spy. We don't want her flying off to report.'

Evie sat up slowly, wary of the short swords pointing in her direction.

'I was flying!' she shouted suddenly, scrambling to her feet and startling those around her. 'Actually flying! How is that possible?' She stopped and stared open-mouthed at the girls, who were now hovering above the ground, their bright, colourful wings spread and beating menacingly.

She twisted around, hoping to feel wings sprouting from her own back, then slumped, saddened to find only the thick material that had kept her aloft.

'Where am I, what is this place?' she whispered.

'Don't tell her anything,' cautioned the older girl. 'She'll only report back to her squad master, you know what those girls from Desert Snake are like. Can't be trusted an inch.'

Evie looked at her, confused. 'But I really don't know

where I am! Or how I got here. Believe me, I've had some very strange experiences recently, anything could be possible! Please, help me out and tell me where we are.'

The girl looked at her, eyebrows raised in disbelief. 'Do me a favour and stop the innocent act. Girls, grab her. We're going to *make* her talk.'

'No!' yelled Evie as her arms were pinned to her sides and a sword pressed against her throat. 'I'm telling the truth. I'm not from this place, I have no idea where I am.'

She looked the girl in the eyes. 'I promise you – I mean you no harm. I just want to go home.'

Clear blue eyes watched her, considering. 'Well, you'd have to be pretty stupid to come in *here* unarmed! I suppose it's possible that they treated you so badly over there that they've made you forget everything.' Under her breath, she added, 'I've heard the rumours.'

Suddenly, she grabbed Evie and spun her around. 'Where are your wings?' she cried. 'What have they done to you? Surely not even the Snakes are so barbaric as to cut them off!'

'I've never had any wings,' replied Evie. 'I told you, I don't belong here. All that stopped me from plummeting to my death is this material.' She opened her arms wide to demonstrate.

'A flightsuit? Only men need one of those! You poor thing, to be born without wings.'

The girl came to a decision. 'I have no idea how you got here, or why, but I don't think you're a Snake. How well can you fight?'

'Fight? With one of those?' replied Evie, nodding to the swords still pointing in her direction. 'I'd chop my own arm off, probably.'

Evie laughed at the shocked faces surrounding her. 'What? Very few people know how to sword fight where I come from.'

'But you must have some weapons training, all girls do. Come, tell us – what is your expertise?'

'None. Really, I can't fight. I go to school to learn about science and history and stuff, not how to use a sword. Although it would certainly be more exciting than double maths.'

Blonde curls bounced as the girl tossed her head impatiently. 'I just don't know what to make of all this. Every girl I know is taught to hold a weapon and fight as soon as they can walk. We live and breathe the art of warcraft.'

Waving her arm contemptuously, she added, 'Only the men go to school to learn the boring stuff. They need to know so they can cook and clean for us, to look after us while we protect them. And you're telling me that you don't do that? You don't do your womanly duty?'

She stopped and sighed. 'Right… Crimson Troops. Go on to weapons practice, let me deal with this. I'll join you once I've decided what to do. Not a word to anyone, you hear me!'

The younger girls filed out, casting sidelong, suspicious glances at Evie as they went.

'I'm Tianna, Crimson Troop subleader,' said the girl, once

the last of them had flown towards a large arena. 'It breaks my heart that you can't fly, it really does. But to believe that you're a girl who can't fight is a step TOO FAR!'

As she shouted the last words, she leaped forward, quick and light on her feet. Before Evie had time to draw breath, her head was jerked back and a dagger pressed tight to her neck.

'Hmm…either you're a good actor or you're telling the truth. That was one of the most basic attacks and you didn't even move! Even a toddler would have known how to avoid me.'

She let Evie go and sheathed her sharp blade. Evie staggered forward and released the breath she had been holding.

'What was that for? I told you I couldn't fight,' she demanded indignantly, putting her hands on her hips.

'It was my duty to make sure,' replied Tianna, serenely.

She looked at Evie in pity. 'I am deeply sorry that you've never flown the dance of death, experienced the elegant beauty of a sword fight in the air. All girls hope to become a master one day, but very few have their natural ability and skills. Most of us are trained to fight together in harmony, so we can at least protect our menfolk from the other squads.'

She paused, then added, 'To be honest, we rarely used to fight each other in anger. We were a peaceful nation, despite our love of the fighting form. But our beloved Mukazi died from an unusual ailment, and a *man* took control of the council! I still don't understand why they let a mere man tell them what to do. Few of us have ever seen him, but now he regularly sends us to battle against the other squads. I've lost many of my sisters and even the younger ones are being sent to war. I'm not even sure what we're fighting for! It's not for the beauty, that's for certain. It's ugly out there, when you're fighting for your life.'

Tianna bit her lip and hung her head, and Evie reached out to comfort her. But the other girl straightened almost immediately.

'We are trained to obey though, so that's what we do. By rights, I should take you straight to my superior. But they don't take kindly to spies, real or not, and I don't want to be the one to send you to your death.'

Evie stared at her, wide eyed. 'What are you going to do with me then?' she asked softly.

Tianna thought for a moment. 'I'm just not equipped to deal with you on my own,' she decided. 'I'm going to take you to a friend of mine.'

She grabbed Evie's hand and led her a battered, wooden hatch set into the mountain. 'Don't worry, I trust her with my life. She'll know what to do.'

Evie followed Tianna down the ladder, ringing footsteps echoing against the stony surfaces of the long shaft. 'It is much further?' she asked, her arms quickly tiring from the unaccustomed activity.

'Not too far,' replied Tianna. 'We never come this way

normally, it's for emergencies only. We usually fly straight down to the lower levels. But I'm not sure your flightsuit is enough for you to make the jump safely, if you're as inexperienced as you seem.'

She stopped, then cursed as Evie stood on her fingers. 'Watch what you're doing!' she cried, standing at the bottom of the shaft and blowing on her painful hands.

'Sorry,' said Evie, climbing down the last few rungs and taking Tianna's hands to rub between her own. 'There, is that better?'

Tianna smiled and put her arm around Evie's shoulders. 'Much better, thanks. Come on, we have a way to go before we reach Anya's quarters. And I don't want anyone to see us on the way.'

She bent down and took off her shoes. 'Quieter that way,' she explained. 'Quick, you do the same.'

She waited impatiently as Evie struggled with the unfamiliar ties, then grabbed her hand and led her down a dark, dank tunnel towards a distant warm glow.

Evie shivered in the cold air as they raced along, trying not to think of the weight of the mountain pressing down. As they approached the end, Tianna put her fingers to her lips, warning Evie to be quiet. Tiptoeing towards to the latticed door that blocked their way, she pressed several of the studs in quick succession. The heavy wood swung open to reveal a brightly lit passageway beyond. Tianna stood for a moment, listening for any people nearby, then gently tugged Evie along to the first of many, bewildering junctions.

'Anya? Anya, are you there? It's me, Tianna. Please let me in, it's urgent,' whispered Tianna, scratching her fingers against the wood of a door. She had made Evie stand at the end of the corridor as a lookout, while she tried Anya's rooms.

'Someone's coming!' whispered Evie urgently, running towards Tianna. 'A man, with a tray of food.'

'Anya! Open up, we need your help now,' begged Tianna with more force, trying the handle of the door. She stumbled forwards as it was yanked open, falling against a tall lady who blocked the entrance. The woman glanced at them both, immediately noting Evie's lack of wings and the sound of someone approaching, and swept them inside without a word.

'Sit,' she commanded, pointing to a long couch lining one side of the spacious room.

Tianna obediently sank into the comfortable cushions, but Evie could only gape at the incredible scenery framed within the clear glass forming one side of the room. Snow-topped mountains rose and fell as far as the eye could see, piercing the mass of clouds above. Green trees dotted the slopes, dwarfed by the incredible crags. She began to edge away from the glass, her head spinning from the sheer scale of the rocky peaks.

'Here, this will help. Drink it while it's hot,' said Anya, handing Evie a mug and gently touching her arm with the intention of steering her towards the seat. They both exhaled sharply as an intense tingling swept through them at the contact. Anya jerked her hand away and stared hard at Evie.

'Where did you come from, did Agathe send you? Has she found me at last?' she demanded, her cool, efficient manner changing instantly to menace.

'Agathe?' said Evie, rubbing her arm where Anya had touched her and backing away from her. 'Who is she?'

'She is the one who did this,' growled Anya, stepping closer and sweeping aside her lustrous hair to reveal a vicious, ugly scar running from her temple and across what remained of an ear.

Evie stared in horror at the puckered, shiny flesh. 'Who would do such a thing?' she said, reaching up to lightly touch the older woman's face. Once again, her skin prickled as the energy flowed between them.

'Don't! warned Anya, roughly pushing Evie's hand away. 'Just…don't. Sit down, let me think for a moment.'

She thrust Evie towards the sofa and stalked over to the window. 'Tell me what is happening,' she demanded, glaring at them both. She pointed to Evie. 'Why are you here, what do you want from me?'

'So you see, I have no real idea *how* I got here! Or why. All I know is that if this is real, then I'm not on Earth anymore,' said Evie.

Tianna had listened in astonishment. 'I didn't really know what else to do, but I'm glad I decided to bring Evie to you,' she said to Anya. 'You know what the squad leaders are like, they certainly wouldn't have believed her. Strangers would *not* have been welcomed after all the upset caused by the new leader taking charge.'

She reached towards Anya and held her hand.

'I know you're also an outsider, Anya, but at least you have wings. You fit in so well with us, you're like one of our own. That last battle you had was incredible! I don't know what we can do about Evie though, who doesn't have wings and doesn't even know how to fight?'

Anya frowned, lost in thought. 'You did the right thing, Tianna,' she said, gently squeezing her hand before letting it drop. 'But there are far more things going on here than you realise. I need to speak to Evie in private. Would you please leave us for a while?'

'You…you won't hurt her, will you?' asked Tianna, nervously. 'She will be safe with you, won't she?'

'As safe as anyone like her is ever going to be,' replied Anya, looking at Evie in sorrow. 'Go on now, leave us. We will talk later.' She ushered Tianna out of the room as Evie sent her a small smile of thanks, laced with uncertainty.

Evie's palms began to sweat as Anya returned and sat next to her.

'Let me try this one more time, just to be sure,' she said, placing her hand over Evie's. She maintained the touch as the energy surged.

Evie's vision began to blur, overlaid with an array of iridescent strands. She had a momentary *understanding* that the strands connected everything, simply everything that existed, before crying out, 'Stop, please! That's enough, it's too much,' She snatched her hand away to cover her face and slumped into the couch.

'You really are new at this, aren't you,' said Anya, moving a short distance away to give her room to recover.

'At what?' cried Evie. 'What is happening to me?'

'You're a naquant, of course. A natural quantum traveller who can navigate the net.'

Evie looked at her in bewilderment. 'Vespera said the same thing, but I have no idea what either of you are talking about.'

'The net is the lifeforce that connects everything,' explained Anya, patiently. 'Naquants like us can sense it, and those of us who are adepts can even visualise it at will. It looks very much like our own nervous system when the nerve cells have been activated, but is mostly energy rather than matter. We can open the quantum channels linking everything and travel along them. We can travel between worlds, between universes! And in time, if it comes to that – time has no meaning in the net.'

Evie closed her eyes, her thoughts chaotic, trying to come to terms with what she was hearing. 'So, is our whole body transported? How do we get back home again?'

'The quantum state of the particles from which you are made becomes entangled with that of particles at your destination. Your consciousness translocates across the resulting channel. Your original atoms lose their form, which can be rather upsetting for anybody watching, so ideally you should be alone when you travel.'

Anya paused, seeing the distress on Evie's face. She lightly stroked her hair to comfort her, the touch sending shivers down Evie's spine.

'Don't worry, my dear,' she reassured her. 'It's a natural process for us, as easy as breathing. When it's time to go home, you will automatically follow the link back to the exact moment you left. If that is what you choose, of course. In reality, we can go anywhere we want, if we are able to open another channel.'

She sat for a moment to let Evie absorb the information, then continued. 'As soon as your task here is finished, you'll be home again in no time.'

'Task, what task? What am I supposed to do?' cried Evie, overwhelmed.

'You will know, when the time comes,' said Anya. 'You'll feel it inside you, a certainty that a particular decision is the right one to make. That's what us naquants do, we help the net flow in the right direction, so life is much easier for everyone.'

'Is that why *you're* here, to do a task?'

Anya's face darkened as she sat quietly. 'No,' she replied after a few moments. 'My naquant days are over. I chose not to travel any longer.'

She sighed, rubbing her face with her hands. 'I used to work for OPOL, as did all naquants. We observed the flow of the net and sensed when certain people had reached a decision that would influence the whole of their society. We can tell which direction is likely to be the most beneficial and tried to guide those people along that path.'

She stopped, her lips curling into a sneer. 'Then Agathe came along and everything changed. She created a device called lifoNET, and now anyone can travel the net. What's more, she uses lifoNET to identify those critical events and change their course in her favour. She has grabbed control of so many worlds!'

'Why doesn't anyone stop her?' asked Evie, bewildered. 'Surely it's easy enough to stop just one person?'

'Oh, we've tried!' exclaimed Anya. 'But when someone as ruthless and controlling as Agathe surrounds herself with selfish, avaricious people who also crave dominance over others, it's surprisingly difficult to get them to give up that taste of power. I think the ability to control others motivates some people far more than money ever could.'

She stood and walked over to the window, absentmindedly gazing at the majestic scenery. 'I gave up when Agathe gave me this,' she said, turning back to Evie and fingering her scar. 'She sent her lackey after me. Despite all my training, I couldn't fight him off. He was too fast, and his knife was too sharp. I managed to escape with my life…but I lost the will to continue after that. Especially when my naquant friends started to disappear.'

Returning to sit next to Evie, she looked into her eyes. 'I still feel the pull of the net, although it is very weak these days. I'm ashamed that I've been too scared to travel. lifoNET can track any surge in the network, and I know Agathe is searching for all remaining naquants. I don't want her to know where I am.' She hesitated, clearly torn.

Biting her lip, she continued. 'Now you've arrived, I think my days of hiding are over. I can *feel* it, despite my fading abilities. You're someone special Evie. I'm terrified, I'll admit it – I don't want to feel pain like that ever again. But I know I must help you, it's the *right* thing to do.'

Decision made, Anya abruptly stood and looked down at Evie.

'Let's get started then,' she said impatiently. 'We need to speak to the council, that much is clear. The flow of the net has been disrupted ever since the Mukazi died. Few of us have ever seen the man who took control, I think it's time to find out why. I've had a gut feeling for a while that Agathe's scheming mind was behind events, but didn't want to draw attention to myself.'

She scowled in annoyance at her weakness. 'Let's make our way to the council chambers and decide what to do when we get there. Come.'

She strode over to the door, Evie scrambling to her feet to follow. 'The main problem, of course, is getting there without being seen. You don't have any wings, which is unheard of for a girl. You're guaranteed to be noticed and most likely arrested. You can't blend in like I can with this lovely pair.'

Anya unfurled her resplendent wings, the pure white feathers glinting in the rays of the sun peeking over the edge of the mountains.

'So beautiful,' Evie whispered, envy gnawing at her. 'I really wish I had some, I loved flying…well, falling through the air.'

'I guess you don't need them to complete your task,' said Anya. 'I, on the other hand, will really miss flying, if I have to move on from this world.'

She stood for a moment, remembering the strength and agility of her wings and the joyful freedom of swooping and gliding through the air.

Sighing, she said, 'We will need to go through the maintenance passageways to reach the chamber. Security is tight these days, guards are always watching for enemy spies. I hope you don't mind enclosed spaces. It will be a bit of a squeeze in places, only room for us and a few spiders.'

Evie looked at her, her heart sinking. 'As long as they aren't bigger than me, I should be able to cope,' she said, shuddering slightly.

Evie swiped at her face again in irritation, the sticky cobwebs clinging everywhere. Groaning in misery, she saw Anya disappearing down yet another side tunnel and crawled tiredly after her.

Her back throbbed where it had scraped the rocky passage above and her fingers and knees were raw. The flightsuit was making her sweat and itch in all kinds of unreachable places and frankly, she just wanted to go home and sleep, forget all about this naquant nonsense. She was too young for it, surely?

She thumped the wall in frustration, wincing at the sharp pain in her already sore knuckles. Tears dripped down her face, leaving streaks in the dust. Feeling lost and alone, and very far from home, Evie longed for a hug from her mom right now.

'Why did you leave me?' she sobbed. 'I miss you so much.'

Pressing her palms down onto the stony surface of the passage, she rested her forehead against the cool rock and cried. As she tried to control her hitches and sniffles, feeling like her heart was breaking, a warm, soothing sensation washed over her. Evie blinked in surprise, her tears forgotten. She gasped as the swell of energy swept her sadness away, leaving her calm and comforted. Her nose caught a scent of lemon and freesias before being overpowered by the sharp tang of the stone surrounding her.

Sniffing and wondering in amazement at what had just happened, she wiped her face and crawled on, determined to catch Anya before she was lost in the warren of stone.

'Shhh…' breathed Anya softly into Evie's ear. 'Make no sound, we should be right above the council chamber now. There's a vent over there, we'll be able to see and hear everything. Be careful where you crawl though, follow me exactly. If we step on a ceiling tile, we'll fall straight through.'

Inching forward, Anya began to crawl towards the opening. Evie followed carefully, wincing at the creaking of her leather flightsuit and trying to calm her harsh breathing, exhausted after the unaccustomed activities. She collapsed in relief as she reached the wider ledge surrounding the vent, then peered through the metal slats into the vast chamber below. Her breath misted in the frigid air as voices drifted up to them.

'Listen,' whispered Anya, brushing her fingers lightly against Evie's arm. 'Lenora is speaking, the deputy leader. Let's hear what she has to say.'

'We need to escalate the fighting, establish control while we have the upper hand. We have to expand our boundaries beyond Storm Valley and into the Flowing Land, perhaps even into the Harsh Country. And we need to do it fast before they can retaliate.' Lenora slammed her fist onto the podium and swept a steely gaze around the room. 'We have already had reports of spies within our midst, we need to move *now* before they become more powerful.'

'But what do we hope to gain, Lenora? What possible reason could justify fighting those who were once our allies?' asked an aged, willowy woman rising from her chair. 'Why should we risk the lives of our girls on what seems to me a reckless whim?'

Looking down her thin nose at her lifelong adversary, Leonora answered, her voice dripping with contempt. 'If you could ever be bothered to attend the meetings, *Adeline*, you would know that our new Mukazi assures us that this is the only way to show devotion to our beloved goddess, Luhunis. He has convinced me that only by entering into glorious battle with our greatest foes – to the death, if necessary – will we be offering the ultimate sacrifice necessary to enter the Sacred Realms.'

Evie watched with interest as Adeline sighed loudly and rolled her eyes.

'You were always so gullible, dear,' she said to Leonora languidly, her shrewd eyes watching for Leonora's reaction. 'It is no secret that I was opposed to appointing a man to the position of Mukazi, and it seems my fears have been justified. We have known nothing but pain and misery since he seized control.'

She slowly walked over to where Leonora was standing, fingers turning white as she gripped the podium.

'How did we manage to get into a situation like this, where we kill rather than protect, where we offer tributes of death rather than the beauty of our flying. Your blind devotion to this man is the main reason why we have fallen this far, Leonora. You and your cronies have accepted the Mukazi's words without ever questioning his motives. I say no more fighting, enough is enough! I vote to revoke the Mukazi's authority right now. Who is with me?'

She turned to face the rest of the council, her arms raised high. In the total silence that followed her rallying cry, Evie could almost hear Adeline's heart sink as she faced row upon row of unconvinced, fearful faces. Slowly, she lowered her arms.

'So be it then. If it is your desire to expand this pointless war, then who am I to stop you? I hereby relinquish my position as council member, as I refuse to kill anyone. Especially based only on the wishes of a man like Emil.'

'Do I hear my name being taken in vain?' drawled a voice from the now open doorway. A huge man bent his head to enter, his silvery blond hair glinting in the bright lights of the council chamber. 'What issue do you have with me now, Adeline, pray tell?'

Evie narrowed her eyes, trying to get a closer look at the looming, half-familiar figure. She turned to Anya, intending to ask if she knew who he was, but exclaimed at the vacant, petrified look in the woman's eyes.

'Anya? Anya? What on earth is the matter? Anya, speak to me'

Anya turned her head, blue eyes wide in her white, strained face. 'It's him! It's…it's Emil. He's come to get me, he's going to kill me this time.'

She grabbed Evie's arms in panic, terror making her fingers dig deep into the skin. 'I don't want that agony again, Evie, you have to help me, please!'

Tears of pain filled Evie's eyes as she tried remove Anya's frantic grip. As she did, she became aware of the net flowing between them and her surroundings became hazy and distant. With a small cry, she moved backwards, taking Anya with her. Their combined weight fell onto the flimsy ceiling tile, and they plummeted towards stone floor of the council chamber.

At the last moment, Anya's wings unfolded to slow their descent and they landed heavily at the feet of the surprised council. Evie opened her eyes to once again find many short swords aimed in her direction. As she lay there, trying to breathe properly after the hard impact, she saw dismay wash over Emil's face at seeing Anya, which turned to utter disbelief when he looked at Evie. Quickly regaining his composure, he smiled humourlessly at them both.

'Explain yourselves,' demanded Leonora angrily. 'Why were you spying on us, who are you working for? Tell us now, or we will gut you where you stand.'

'I doubt you could ever harm me, Leonora,' said Anya, using her wings to gracefully stand, unceremoniously pulling Evie up with her. 'You are all much too slow to ever best me.'

Adeline pushed through the bristling weapons to stand before Anya and look searchingly into her eyes.

'Tell us the truth, Anya, what is happening here?' she asked gently after a moment, noting the fearful determination in her face. 'You are a trusted and valued friend, but your actions do look rather suspicious, you have to admit.'

Anya took a deep breath, held it for a moment, then released it explosively. 'I accuse this man of lying to you all, of trying to control our world for his own purposes. Or at least, those of the foul woman whose orders he so willingly obeys. Not until I saw his face here for the first time did I realise who he was. He is the man who did *this* while he was trying to kill me!'

She defiantly swept aside her heavy hair to display the brutal scar. The women around her gasped in shock and as one looked at Emil, expecting to hear his denial.

"Well, well, well. If it isn't my dear old friend Anya. Who would have expected to see you here, of all places? And with little Evie as well. How fortunate for me, Agathe will be most happy. You know full well the consequences of displeasing our illustrious leader, Anya.' He stopped, and sighed. 'I think my time here is done, Evie is far more important.'

With those words, he sprang forward to grab Evie, who shrank back in terror. Anya, who had been watching Emil closely and saw when his body tensed to pounce, jumped in front of her and pushed her behind for protection.

'Run Evie, you must get out of here,' she shouted, grappling with Emil and using her muscular wings to keep him off balance. She half-turned her head to look at Evie, momentarily losing concentration, then gave a strange, gurgling cry as Emil slowly pulled out a sharp dagger from beneath her ribs. A splash of red marred the white perfection of her wings as the blood gushed from her lifeless body.

Evie screamed as she felt Anya's lifeforce drain into the net, caressing her mind before swirling away into the endless network. Heartbroken, Evie stood paralysed, the tears coursing down her face, watching Emil struggle against the restraining hands of the shocked council. The spell broke and she flung herself towards Emil, shouting with rage, intent on revenge.

Before she could reach him, her small body was held back by the strong embrace of Adeline.

'Don't let Anya die in vain,' she whispered urgently into Evie's ear. 'He clearly wants you, so I refuse to let him have you. You must flee, escape somehow. We will hold him here and deal with him, never fear. His time here is indeed done. Anya's death is tragic, but this will change the course of our world. We still have time to undo all the damage he has caused, we will have peace again. But for now, go! Our strength is with you.'

With these words, Adeline thrust Evie towards the open chamber door. Evie sobbed as she once again saw Anya's slumped body looking so small and broken. Yet despite her sadness, she had a sudden certainty that Anya's death had been the only thing that could have turned the council against Emil. *If this was the only way,* she thought, *I'm not sure I'm going to like being a naquant.* With a final searing glance in Anya's direction, she turned and ran for freedom.

Struggling against the seasoned fighters surrounding him, their strength magnified by their anger, Emil saw Evie race away. *No, she must not escape again, Agathe will kill me. Or worse.* He redoubled his efforts to free himself, before resigning himself to capture.

'I surrender!' he called out to Leonora, who was always

his closest ally. 'Lenora, you know me. You know I wouldn't have done this without a very good reason. Get your women to unhand me and I'll explain everything.'

He smiled winningly at the tall, spare woman, his eyes sparkling, and watched in satisfaction as her sour face softened. *Too easy*, he gloated to himself.

'Let him go,' she ordered, walking over to where he stood. 'Let him have his say and then we will decide what to do with him.'

'Are you mad, woman?' cried Adeline in amazement. 'He has killed one of us, within our own chambers! You can't trust him, surely?'

'Much as I admired Anya, she was not one of us. For all we know, she might have been a hardened criminal before she came here. I am the deputy leader, and I say that Emil should be allowed to speak freely.'

Leonora looked at Emil and laid her hand on his arm. 'Why was it so necessary to kill Anya, please tell me?' she implored softly, her light, tender touch irritating Emil's already heightened senses. He put his hand firmly over Leonora's wrist, the warmth causing her to smile gently.

'Oh, I didn't have to kill her, Leonora. I wanted to. And now it's your turn.'

Leonora's smile turned to horror as Emil pulled down on her unresisting arm, onto the sharp knife angled towards her body. Flinging her away without a second glance, Emil grabbed the neural disruptor from the folds of his robe and fired on those descending upon him like wild furies. They fell like stones from air until he was the only one left standing. Breathing heavily, he felt a fleeting despair at the certain punishment to be inflicted by Agathe at losing control of another world. With a fatalistic shrug, he loped away to chase Evie to ground.

How do I get out of this place? thought Evie frantically, panting as she stumbled along yet another rocky corridor. *I'm never going to get out of here. Surely the task has been completed now, why am I still here?*

She stopped and bent over to catch her breath, wiping the sweaty hair from her face. As she did, a heavyset man appeared around the corner and called out to her.

'Boy! Why are dawdling? Shouldn't you be helping in the kitchens at this time of day? Come here, let me see what Division you're from.'

He strode up to Evie and caught her arm. His face paled at the sight of the wingless girl. 'What is the meaning of this, you're no boy! Where are your wings?' His hand trembled. 'This needs to be reported at once. Guards? Guards! We have an intruder, arrest her.'

Knowing she had no choice, Evie sank her teeth deep into his meaty hand. She winced at his pained cry, but also at the strong taste of garlic saturating his skin. As he released her, clutching his fingers, she stamped on the arch of his foot and darted away, leaving him hopping in agony.

She ran to the end of the corridor, which opened out into

a large plaza. Behind her lumbered the irate, injured man, still crying out for the guards. At the other end of the massive room, she could see a commotion, people milling around. Towering over everyone was Emil, urging them to look everywhere. He glanced over towards Evie, and bellowed.

'There she is! Grab her. She is the one who has killed two council members. Look, she has no wings, like I told you. She is a spy, sent to kill and disrupt. I want her now…alive, so she can be properly punished.'

The will drained out of Evie as she watched the mob approach. She had nowhere to go, no-one to help her, and she'd had enough of running. She stood there, drooping, waiting for the inevitable to happen. A sharp, insistent voice broke through her apathy.

'Hey, down here, quick. You must hurry before they reach you.'

Evie looked down to someone peering through a grille in the floor. Once side of his face was covered with a purpling yellowish bruise.

'Hurry,' he urged. 'They're almost upon us. Climb in, they're too big to follow.'

He lifted the grille and tugged on the leg of her flightsuit. Scrambling quickly, she lowered herself through the narrow opening. The boy slammed the grille shut, sliding the bolt to lock it. He turned towards her and smiled, bright white teeth flashing against warm, tawny skin. He brushed some dust from his sliver hair.

'That should keep them busy for a little while, but we

need to get to the surface. You aren't meant to be here, you can't wander these corridors forever, you know. Follow me, I know the way.'

'It…it's you!' exclaimed Evie, recognising her rescuer from the park. 'But who are you? And how on earth did you get here?'

'I'm Finn. But there's no time for explanations now,' he replied, impatiently. 'Some other time, I'm sure. We need to get moving, come on.'

With that, he crawled off through the air flow duct. Her knees already throbbing at the thought, Evie tiredly followed.

Emil cursed loudly as once again that fool boy helped Evie to escape. He would need to do something about him soon. Thinking furiously, he tried to work out where they might be heading. It seemed Evie had only recently discovered her naquant abilities, and he knew her quantum state would require a severe shock to send it back to its original state. With a cry of triumph, he knew where the boy would be taking her.

He forced his way through the crowds, over to the passage that led up to the flying ledges. There was only one near this plaza, they would be headed there. He pulled out his disruptor in preparation, knowing he would only get one chance. Thinking ahead, he also set his el-VA to lifoNET headquarters. His hours of training kicked in as he quickly ran up the steep slope, his breath even and heart beating strong and steady.

Unaware, the thrill of the chase and potential prize made his lips curl wolfishly over his teeth, marring his handsome face. He was getting close, he was sure. He just hoped he wasn't too late.

'There you go,' said Finn, pulling Evie from the hole in the side of the mountain. She tumbled out onto the rocky ledge, weak from exertion.

'I can't take any more of this,' she gasped, lying on her back and staring at the gloriously blue sky above.

'You won't have time for anything else ever again if you don't translocate before Emil gets here,' he said, taking hold of her flightsuit and yanking her to her feet. 'Come on, the only way to get home is to jump. The shock will send you back, until you can work out how to do it by yourself.'

Evie stared at him in disbelief as he dragged her towards the edge.

'I'm not throwing myself off there, I'll die!'

'No, you won't, there's no chance of that. Naquants only die if most of their energy has been drained. Or it can leak away if they don't use it. If someone tries to kill a full naquant, all that happens is that their quantum state is sent elsewhere.'

Evie's heart lifted in hope. 'So Anya is still alive somewhere?'

'I don't know who she is. But if her body 'disappeared'

once she'd been killed, then yes, she is still alive.'

Remembering the lifeless body of Anya lying in the chamber, her heart sank, and she bit her lip to stop herself crying.

'I guess she'd stayed here too long,' she said, shaking her head in sorrow.

A loud mocking voice carried across the still air.

'Where are you going to go now, girlie. There's no escape this time, you're coming with me.'

Her adrenalin surged as she saw the tall figure approach from an open passage, strange devices in each hand. She backed up towards Finn, edging closer and closer to the steep drop, not knowing what to do.

'Don't worry,' he said, soothingly. 'Trust me, you won't come to any harm.'

He gently touched her cheek, the touch sending a now familiar tingle through her entire body. Eyes widening in shock, she reached out towards him, then screamed loudly as he pushed her firmly over the edge.

'There's no place like home!' he called to her rapidly disappearing body, a playful grin on his face.

He turned just as Emil launched towards him with a roar, bundling them both over the ledge. Grappling mid-air, they rapidly gained on Evie's tumbling body.

'No more interference from you, boy,' screamed Emil as the wind tore past them. 'It ends now.'

His anger turned to frustration as Finn stuck out his tongue and disappeared.

'Damn all naquants!' cried Emil.

Turning his focus towards Evie, he aimed his disruptor at her head and fired. Then violently cursed as she faded away, realising he'd shocked her home. After a moment of free fall, blessedly peaceful, he sighed. Gathering his will to face the wrath of Agathe, he activated his el-VA and dissolved.

…CONNECTING…

Back in his quarters he paced nervously, wondering how to break the news to Agathe. Anya was dead, no longer a potential source to power lifoNET. He'd lost control over the world, which was bad news after his last unfortunate visit to Aranea, when Vespera had threatened to eat him slowly, limb by limb, after deceiving them all. And the final indignity, he'd lost Evie…again! He didn't dare admit that this was the second time, he valued his sanity too much. He was tough, but the calculating cruelty of the diminutive woman terrified him.

Knowing there was only one person who could ever soothe his fears, he abruptly left his room and furtively made his way to the lifoNET pods. He'd long ago worked out how to gain access to the locked room, with Agathe none the wiser. Slipping inside, he tentatively walked over to Ellen's capsule and gazed at the still form within. His heart quickened at her soft features, saddened by the slack expression that had replaced her lively curiosity and laughter. *I'll never forgive Liam for taking her from me,* he thought, tenderly stroking the clear plastic. *He might be dead, but I still hate him. I hope he suffered in there.*

Lost in memories, he didn't hear soft footsteps approach.

'Reminiscing again, are we Emil? I've been watching you, daydreaming over Ellen again. I thought I'd beaten that weakness out of you a long time ago.'

Emil started violently and whirled around. Agathe stood there watching, an amused sneer on her face.

'She never cared about you, Emil. You were nothing to her. You *are* nothing, you should know that by now.'

Agathe's eyes glinted with malice as Emil struggled to control his anger.

'Report!' she barked suddenly. 'What happened? And don't lie, lifoNET detected the surges.'

Emil straightened and bowed his head, unable to look her in the eyes.

'I failed. Anya is dead and I lost control of the council.'

There was absolute silence as Agathe watched him closely.

'What else?' she asked, the coolness of her tone making Emil lick his suddenly dry lips.

He gathered his courage. 'Evie was there, she's discovered her abilities. She escaped, with the help of the boy.'

His blood ran cold when he finally found the nerve to

look at Agathe. Instead of the raging hot fury he'd expected to see, her face was rigid with icy malevolence.

Slowly and deliberately, Agathe walked up to Ellen's capsule. 'Such a pretty thing, so full of life. I think she'll be the one to pay for your incompetence.'

Laughing cruelly at Emil's horrified understanding, Agathe turned the dial to maximum to extract more energy.

'No,' cried Emil helplessly, as the faint lines on Ellen's face deepened and spread and her lustrous dark hair began to turn white.

After a moment of watching his agony, her eyes narrowed in enjoyment, Agathe turned down the dial.

'We don't want to drain her of all energy just yet, not until I can replace her with someone younger and stronger. But if you fail me again, Ellen won't be the only one to suffer. Kneel down, I want to give you a reminder.'

As the tall man knelt reluctantly before her, Agathe clutched his face in a vice-like grip, sharp nails digging deep.

'Don't move,' she warned, before taking a small, wickedly sharp knife and slowly tracing the skin around his eye.

Despite the pain, Emil kept still as the line of blood began to drip.

'If you lose her again, you will lose the eye. I promise you that. And that will be just the beginning. I want Evie and I need her alive. Do you think you can do that for me?'

Emil nodded carefully, flinching as the point of the unwavering knife came perilously close to his eyeball.

Agathe nodded, satisfied, and released him. Turning her

back on him, disregarding any threat he might pose, she walked towards the door.

'You should have remembered that naquants often visit our worlds to try and undo our work. Please set your el-VA to alert you of any surges in those regions. There aren't many free naquants left. One of them is bound to be Evie.'

She stopped and looked back at him. 'You know, of course, that they rarely have a relationship, it is too intense. And they never had any children, until now. The love between Liam and Ellen must have been great indeed to overcome those problems.'

She laughed in delight at the pain that crossed Emil's face at her words, and at the hatred in his eyes.

'The potential in Evie is huge, Emil. She alone could power lifoNET. Besides which, I am sure Liam will have told her where the plans are, or at least how to get them, and I want them back. I refuse to let anyone destroy my creation.' She stood for a moment, fists clenched.

'Find her,' she ordered, and stalked away, leaving Emil wiping blood from his face.

Finn nestled deeper into the bushes and wrapped the thin, worn blanket around him, trying to escape the cold winds whistling through the park. He could feel the sharp edges of an el-VA pressing into his side, stolen in the knowledge he had to keep it safe, and he shifted position again.

He'd been somewhat dismayed to find himself back in the

park after falling through the sky with Emil. Clearly, the girl still needed his protection. Lately, he seemed destined to travel wherever Emil was likely to turn up, he couldn't deny the link between them. He knew he'd have to find a better way to protect her against him.

He cautiously touched his bruise, still sore after Emil had thrown him face first into the tree. He supposed it added an authentic touch to his character when he was out stealing food. Sighing deeply, he began to chew on a half-eaten burger he'd seen someone throw away, and waited patiently for Emil to arrive.

3. THE CHOICES WE MAKE

'It is the still, small voice that the soul heeds, not the deafening blasts of doom.'

—*William Dean Howells*

Even a couple of days later, Evie found her hands trembling when she thought of that wild fall from the mountain. She'd arrived back in the armchair, her book still in her lap, just as Anya had said.

Breathing deeply, head between her knees, she had tried to calm her racing heart and mind. Tears leaked from tightly closed lids as she longed for a hug from Aaron. If he hadn't been at work, she would have sobbed out a confusing account of what was happening to her. But by the time he'd returned home that evening, the urge to talk had faded.

Aaron, I can travel between worlds to help people make decisions. I've already met some giant spiders and flying women. Oh, and there's a big man who's trying to capture me and a boy who seems to be protecting me. She could quite clearly imagine his look of disbelief, concern at her mental state of mind, and a gentle suggestion to see a counsellor to 'talk things over'. But then she remembered his warnings that her mom had been killed, and guilt washed over her at keeping this secret. *If it happens again, I really will tell him everything,* she promised herself.

In the meantime, she'd been keeping busy. She'd promised Aaron she would tidy the garden during the holidays, and weeding furiously had kept the worst of her fears at bay. Back aching, she stretched in the warm afternoon air and decided to sweep up the rapidly wilting stalks.

Walking over to the dilapidated shed, she opened the door and walked into the musty-smelling gloom, the stored heat of the day making her curls cling to her forehead. She swiped at her face in irritation, coughing and sneezing in the dusty air, and vainly scrabbled around for the broom as her eyes tried to adjust to the dark. She yelped in pain as she banged her head on a shelf and stood still, blinking back tears and gritting her teeth, trying to be patient.

As her breathing slowed, she gazed at the motes of dust caught in the weak beam of sunlight leaking through a gap in the boards. She felt her mind begin to loosen its hold and had a brief moment to register the infinite web of sparkling threads linking endless, brightly burning nodes, before the incredible force sucked her mind into the void and flung it towards a distant, flickering point.

She opened her eyes to see a winged nightmare flying towards her, fangs flashing and claws outspread, screeching a guttural shriek. With an embarrassingly high squeal of surprise, Evie scrabbled backwards across the stone floor, flailing her arms to fend off the creature. As it drew closer, she saw her opportunity and kicked out with a satisfying thud.

She groaned in pain as her boot connected with what felt like solid stone. Rolling around in agony, she yelled in fright as huge, vice-like hands grabbed her and lifted her high into the air.

'Where is he?' screamed the monster, spraying greyish spit over Evie's face.

She shuddered in revulsion but managed to stammer a reply. 'Who are you talking about, I don't even know where I am!'

'Our Mason, what have you done with him? If you have hurt him, I will rip you apart,' threatened the dark apparition, putting a razor-sharp talon to her throat.

She grew pale, then cried out as she was violently shaken. Her teeth still rattling, she yelled, 'Stop, please stop! Just put me down so I can help you.'

The creature paused and looked at her more closely.

'You're just a girl. Are you with those thieves? I will break your bones if you are.' He shook her again warningly.

Evie scowled indignantly. 'No more shaking, I've had enough. I am *not* a thief.'

He slowly lowered her to the floor, where she collapsed in a heap.

'Who are you then?' he asked, curiously. 'Why are you here?'

'I'm Evie,' she explained, wiping her fringe from her face and looking up with stormy blue eyes. 'I travelled through the web...or net. Whatever it's called. I guess I'm here to help?'

Confusion spread across his terrible face, followed by resignation.

'I know not of what you speak,' he sighed. 'It matters not. You are but a young girl. And an ugly one at that. What use will you be?'

Evie bristled at being called ugly by a hideous beast, but replied, 'If you tell me who you are and what the problem is, maybe I can help you?'

'Well,' said the monster, drawing himself up to his fullest, most dignified height and wrapping his wings round his misshapen body. 'I am Daryn, Most High of the Babewyn, Lord Protector of all who dwell within this castle and its grounds.'

'You look like a giant gargoyle to me,' smirked Evie. She stepped back in alarm as Daryn hissed furiously.

'I am *not* a gargoyle, you ignorant wretch! I am pure chimera. Do you see water spouting from my mouth?'

Evie sniggered, then coughed slightly and gestured for Daryn to continue.

'I am responsible for the safety of all who live here in Hordrig Castle,' he declared haughtily.

Evie blinked in surprise at hearing the familiar name,

remembering several trips to the local castle. She wondered if Anya was right after all, naquants could travel in time. That didn't explain a seven-foot tall stone monster, but she was beginning to believe that anything was possible. Her thoughts returned to the present and her eyes rested on Daryn, arms crossed and looking increasingly annoyed by her inattention.

'I'm sorry Daryn, your words triggered an important memory,' she soothed. 'Please tell me more.'

He looked at her reproachfully, then resumed. 'Tonight is a blood moon, the only time when our Master Mason can give life to a new, true Babewyn like myself. He was halfway through creating what was to be my life mate, when he was attacked and dragged away by some filthy thugs.'

Daryn looked down in shame and added, 'I was keeping watch on the roof, as is my duty, but I didn't see them sneak in. I failed, and this is my punishment.'

With his head hanging, he slowly lifted his arm to point at a dark, sinister lump deep in the shadows of the cold and draughty room.

Evie shivered as she drew closer, the hairs on the back of her neck quivering as she entered the darkness. From the depths of a huge chunk of rock, a twisted form was clearly trying to escape but was frozen within. The tormented expression on the sculpture's face made Evie's blood run cold, a look of horror and desperation at being trapped between life and non-life within the rock.

With a tremor in her voice, she whispered, 'We need to

free it, we can't leave it like that!'

'No, we cannot,' replied Daryn fiercely. 'I need to find where those men took the Mason so he can release my mate. I need to do it fast, before the moon sets.'

His face twisted in anguish as he snarled, 'I don't know where to find him though! The Mason knows all the secrets of this castle, including the location of the treasure room. But he is a dutiful man, he has always refused to tell anyone where it is, apart from the owner of the castle. I'm afraid they might be trying to torture the information out of him.'

Daryn paused, his head bent. When he looked up, Evie stepped back at the fury and violence in the chimera's face. 'When I find them, I will tear them apart if they have hurt my Mason.'

Evie crept along the dark, dusty corridor, flinching at every scuttle of insect feet and magnified shadow from her spluttering torch. Daryn was gallumping ahead, excitedly leading the way after she had persuaded him with a demonstration of her emerging naquant abilities.

'Describe the Mason to me,' Evie had demanded earlier, placing her hand on the distorted sculpture, wondering if the net could help her.

'He is short, powerfully muscled, dark thinning hair, with a jaw that is squarer even than mine,' he replied at once.

Evie looked up at Daryn's jutting chin and raised an eyebrow at the vision it conjured up. Closing her eyes and concentrating hard on his description, she tried to visualise the web like Anya had said, sensing it just *below* normality. Gradually, the network stuttered into view, superimposed over the stone surfaces surrounding them. Evie shivered slightly as her hair stood on end.

'Give me more details,' she asked gently. 'What is he *like*?'

Daryn stood still, his expressive eyes screwed up in thought. 'Honest. Honest and brave, always determined to do the right thing. And kind, even to one such as me.' Shaking his head sadly he had looked at her, first in the hope that she could help, and then in consternation as he saw her standing stock still with her head moving from side to side as though searching for something, eyeballs rolling beneath their lids.

'I can sense him,' she cried. 'His node is weak, but I can see the strands connecting us to him. This is incredible! Quick, what can I use to make a map?'

Evie had sprung into action, scratching lines onto the stone floor with the abandoned chisel Daryn handed to her. 'This is us, and this is the direction we must take. But how do we get from here to there through these thick walls? I could try and travel the net, but I am not sure I can take you with me.'

'Follow me,' Daryn commanded, deciding in an instant to trust her. 'I know this place almost as well as the Mason himself. I will lead the way.'

Which is how she found herself creeping along the corridors, trying to keep up with Daryn's long stride while avoiding the sinister clutches of creeping, crawly things. She was no longer so fond of spiders after watching the Araneans eat. Taking a deep breath and gathering her courage, she sped up after the chimera's retreating back.

'He should be right here, I can feel him!' said Evie, spinning round in confusion, smoke from the torch swirling around with her. She had followed Daryn ever downwards until she'd detected the Mason nearby, then had led the way, following the strand to his exact location – a dank, dark passageway closed at one end, with no Mason in sight.

'Well, clearly he's not here,' said Daryn dismissively, to her annoyance. 'Seems you're not much help after all.'

Evie seethed, then realization struck. 'His node is right under my feet. He must be in a room below us.'

'There is nothing below but solid rock,' said Daryn. 'We have reached the bottom of the castle, which was built on a mountain of stone. We cannot go any lower.'

'You said he was a Master Mason who knew all the secret rooms and passageways. The treasure room must be below us,' she said, excitedly. 'Look around for any way of opening the door.'

While Daryn knocked on the walls and floor and pressed everything in sight, Evie closed her eyes to see if there was any trace of the Mason apart from the node. High up in the corner of the passageway, she noticed a faint, flickering tendril.

'Up there, quick, I can't reach. Push on that dent in the ceiling.'

Daryn stretched his long, sinuous arm and delicately pressed the hollow in the stone. Rolling her eyes, Evie watched as he tried again and again to force his massive finger into the small spot, getting angrier and more frustrated with each attempt.

'Stop, you'll break it,' she ordered, eventually losing patience. 'Lift me up, I'll do it.'

Holding her more firmly than was strictly necessary, Daryn shot her up into the air, only stopping when her head was jammed up against the hard rock. Evie scowled but decided against kicking Daryn's solid body again. She pressed hard on the hollow and with a click and whirr of hidden, well-oiled mechanisms, a stone slab descended slowly into the floor then slid back to reveal stairs leading down into the dark. A whiff of damp, stony air drifted up – along with the soft thwack of a fist hitting flesh and a low grunt of pain.

'Err, you first,' said Evie, hurriedly moving behind Daryn's massive body. Needing no encouragement, he charged down the stairs, roaring with rage.

'Where is it, where is the door to the treasure room?' demanded the thin, unkempt man crouching over a bruised and battered man lying on the floor. 'We won't stop until we get what we deserve.'

'You deserve this!' screeched Daryn, grabbing him and

flinging him across the room. With a sickening crunch, he slumped against the wall. The two men holding down the Mason looked at each other, then leaped towards the stairs, pushing each other out of the way in their attempt to flee. Grabbing each around the neck with his massive, stony hands, Daryn knocked their heads together, then threw them on the floor where they lay motionless. Face drained of all blood, the final man cowered, begging Daryn not to hurt him.

Evie had watched in amazement as Daryn dispatched the men, then exclaimed, 'No Daryn, leave this one alone. We need some answers and they can't say anything if they've all been knocked out. Put your fists away.'

Breathing heavily, wisps of what looked suspiciously like smoke writhing from his nostrils, he settled back on his haunches and refrained from tearing into the terrified man. Bringing himself under control, Daryn looked at him and asked menacingly, 'Why did you hurt my friend. Answer me true, or you will pay.'

The man blanched further, terrified by the living fiend. He gulped. 'We need to know where the treasure room is. Prince Ardan took everything from us and we have nothing left. Our children are starving, the crops are dying, and we are desperate.' He stifled a sob as he continued, 'We didn't want to hurt the Mason, but he wouldn't tell us where it was. We got carried away because we know the Prince will be back from his hunt soon.'

Daryn looked at him, considering. 'Did you tell the

Mason this before you started beating him up? How can I believe a word you say?' His rage flared and he bellowed, 'I ought to rip your head off and be done with it.'

All hope left the man's face as he replied. 'Go ahead then, do it. We don't have much left to live for anyway.' He straightened his back and stared right into Daryn's eyes, waiting for the final blow.

Evie had been watching closely, not just at the scene before her, but also at the web beneath. As the man spoke, his node had stayed clear and bright.

'He's telling the truth, Daryn, he really is. We need to speak to the Mason quickly, see if he can help.'

Rushing over to the prone man, she softly touched his bloodied face. 'He's unconscious. Daryn, go and see if there is any water to wake him.'

'I can do better than that,' declared Daryn, as he bent over the small man's form and *breathed* into his face. The Mason shuddered violently. *I would have done the same,* thought Evie as he sat up, groaning.

'What happened?' he wondered, 'Where am I?' Remembrance dawned when he looked around, the memories flooding back. He looked quickly at the man who had hurt him.

'Why?' he asked simply.

Looking away in shame, the man replied, 'You were our only hope, our last resort, and you wouldn't help us.'

'Help you with what, stealing the treasure? Why would I do that? I swore to keep the room secret when the castle was first built, and I don't break my promises – especially for common thieves who like hurting people.'

Evie touched the Mason's hand, then told him why the men had attacked him.

He looked at the man reproachfully, 'I could have helped you if I had known who you were. I know only too well how badly the Prince has been treating his people. My own nephew was strung up because he took a chicken from the castle kitchen to feed his family. The strange thing is, nobody knows where the Prince came from, or even if he is a prince at all. He appeared one day, assumed control, and not a single person has had the courage to stand up to him. He is a powerful brute of a man who delights in cruelty. I don't think any of that treasure is rightfully his.'

He stopped and thought. Then, with a strange sorrow in his eyes, he came to a decision.

'I may have promised never to reveal where the treasure room is. But I have no reason to keep that treasure away from those to whom it rightfully belongs. I will help you.'

Standing up and swaying a little, he ordered, 'Go back up the stairs, and take those men with you. I don't want you to see the location of the treasure room. That way, I can keep my vow at least. I will bring out all the treasure that I can, then we will have to flee quickly. The Prince will be back at dawn – and I need to finish the sculpture before the moon sets!' he added, looking at Daryn in dismay.

Grabbing one of the fallen men under the arms, he gestured for Evie to take the legs and they carried him up the stairs, Daryn following with a man under each arm. The final man stood for a second, eyes wide open in joyful relief, then traipsed up the stairs behind them.

After releasing his burden, the Mason turned and said, 'Meet me in the woods outside the castle, near the giant oak tree. Be quiet, as the Prince's men might be around. I will be as fast as I can.'

With that, he went back down the stairs and pressed something so that they disappeared, making the floor whole once again. After a short while, they heard a quiet rumble beneath their feet as the Mason opened the treasure room. In readiness to run to the forest, Daryn roused the unconscious men and demanded their names, still not quite ready to forgive them over their treatment of the Mason, despite their good intentions.

'Two wrongs never make a right,' he warned, threateningly.

The man called Will stood tall before Daryn and apologised again.

'You are right. We should have never hurt the Mason, and we are sorry. We wanted so much to change our lives for the better. To use the treasure to feed our families, but also to rise up against this wicked man. To drag him back to the mud where he belongs. To get justice for the way he has treated us.' He stopped, breathing heavily. 'I can only hope that we are successful, so that our own wrong deeds might be atoned.'

Daryn sighed, relenting. 'Come on then, let's get out of

here quickly.' After a quick glance to make sure all were ready to follow, he set off at a quick pace through the maze of corridors.

Breath steaming thickly in the frigid air, Evie stamped her feet to get the blood flowing. They had made it through the underbelly of the castle without any incidents – if you didn't count the five men they had stumbled across, each of whom Daryn had knocked out with a single blow.

Now they were waiting in the cold night, starting at every noise in the forest and watching hopefully for the Mason to arrive. The blood moon hung low in the starry sky, and Evie could see Daryn growing more and more impatient as the time to release his life mate grew shorter. Hunger pangs began to plague her, and she realised she'd had nothing to eat for many hours. Her mind began to drift.

Slowly, she became aware of a faint rustling that grew louder as something heavy was dragged across the leafy ground.

'Quick,' hissed the Mason, hauling a small cart loaded with heavy bags of treasure. 'We don't have much time. Take this and don't waste it. Make every coin count and bring down that Prince.' He passed the handles of the cart to the men, who began tugging it away.

As the cart rumbled past Evie, she gasped, alerted by a pull from the net. 'Wait!' she cried, clinging on to one of the men. 'I must have a look in that bag, please.'

They halted, puzzled, as she clawed open the burlap sack, ignoring Daryn's frantic appeals to hurry. Inside, nestled on a bed of satin, was a beautifully worked silver ring with a strange, flat disc on the top, ridged down the centre. As she picked it up to take a closer look, her fingers tingled with energy, just as they had when she had picked up her mother's items. Examining it more closely, she saw tiny words inscribed on the underside of the plate, impossible to read in the gloom of the woods.

Turning around, she asked, 'Do any of you recognise this?'

Everyone slowly shook their heads.

'Do you mind if I keep it? I have a feeling it's important.' She looked imploringly at the men staring at her.

Will grinned, 'Please take it, we won't miss it.' Turning to the Mason, gratitude shining in his eyes, he added, 'Thank you, my friend. You have risked your life for us, and we will never forget you. 'Ethan the Master Mason' will be a name that we will pass on to our children. Be safe and goodbye.'

With a gap-toothed smile, he slipped silently into the shadows.

Creeping quietly through the dark corridors, using secret passageways revealed by the Mason whenever they heard noise ahead, they made their way back through the silent castle. With increasing urgency as the moon fell ever lower, Daryn herded them along until at last, the sculpture lay before the Mason, waiting for the final stokes of his chisel. The Mason breathed deeply, seeming to *reach* inside himself, then continued with his work.

Evie watched in fascination as the newest member of the Babewyn was finally revealed, each stroke of the chisel executed perfectly. Daryn hovered anxiously like an expectant father, until the Mason brushed him away impatiently. Almost beside himself, Daryn sagged to the floor to wait. Sidling up to him, Evie took his huge, rough hand into her small ones and squeezed tightly. He smiled in thanks and settled down to wait.

Just as the moon was about to set, and Daryn about to explode with worry, the Mason sat back and exhaled.

'She is finished,' he declared with satisfaction. 'Now we wait for the first rays of the sun. Quick, open the shutters.'

Evie ran to the tall window and flung wide the wooden coverings. As she did, the sun flooded the room with light, falling straight onto the finished sculpture. The stone began to ripple along its length and the creature moved as the light grew stronger. Her eyes opened sleepily, and she stretched and yawned.

'I'm awake, at last,' she cried. 'I thought I was never going to be freed.' She looked at the Mason gratefully. 'I thank you from the depths of my soul for releasing me. I am Mila of the Babewyn. Am I the only one of my kind yet awoken?'

Daryn emerged from the shadows, where he had been watching in wonder and trepidation. 'I am Daryn,' he said, almost timidly. 'Your companion – if you will have me?'

Mila looked at him, considering. Then held out her hands to grasp Daryn and hug him with a fierce intensity. Daryn squeezed back, his face full of joy and relief, bonding with his mate. The Mason looked on proudly and Evie couldn't stop herself grinning in delight.

'This must be it,' she thought to herself, 'I'll be going home soon.' But the Mason's node was still spluttering, and she looked around in confusion.

'Something's still not right,' she said. 'The net hasn't been restored. What have we missed?'

Daryn and Mila reluctantly parted to look at her questioningly. As they did, the Mason held up his hand for silence. 'Quiet, can you hear that? Horses and many men. The Prince has returned! If he finds you here, he will take a hammer to the Babewyn and destroy them, then hang me for sorcery. We must get to safety now.'

Springing into action, they dived for the door. Not far from their room, they heard shouting as the soldiers discovered the men knocked out by Daryn. Evie looked at the others.

'They will be here soon. We need a distraction, so you can escape. I will find them and lure them away.'

Although the thought terrified her, it felt *right* to Evie. It was something she had to do to save the others. With a quick hug, shared smile and a final farewell, she turned and headed in the direction of the rough and ready voices.

Breathing heavily, Evie stopped. Her plan had worked, and the soldiers had given chase after the heavy vase she'd flung had hit one of them in the back of the head. She was fast, but she was slowing as she headed up the seemingly endless flights of stairs. She reached the top and found the door to the roof standing open. Not for the first time, she wondered why she had come this way as there was no escape.

Too late to worry now, she ran off again as the bearded, grizzled face of a soldier appeared on the roof. At his shoulder, a large man appeared, breathing heavily. Seeing her, he straightened and pushed away the mane of pale blond hair plastered to his face by sweat. A heavy robe hung from his wide shoulders, richly embroidered and edged in fine, golden fur. He turned to the soldier and whispered urgently into his ear.

Evie watched him, disbelievingly. *It can't be him again, how is that possible?* She tried to make out his features, but the light of the rising sun blinded her. Tearing her eyes away from the leader, she gasped in alarm as she realised the soldiers had crept closer to her unawares.

'Come here, little brat. You can't escape. Boys, fan out, so she can't get past us.'

Boosted by a surge of fear, Evie turned and raced away, heart thumping as she looked around for a means of escape. Her heart sank as she saw nothing but the edge of the roof. Slowing down, she crept closer to the edge, her mouth drying at the sight of the ground so far, far away. She turned to face the soldiers, keeping a close eye on the robed man.

'We have you now,' leered the soldier, 'The Prince here wants a word with you. We have a little room especially for prisoners like you. You'll love it, as long as you're not too attached to those pretty little fingernails of yours.'

Evie's eyes went wide. There was no way she was going to be tortured, especially if Emil was here. *But that's impossible!* Looking around, she climbed onto the parapet, an idea beginning to form. It had worked before and if Finn was right, she should be safe enough. With a last fleeting hope that the others had made it to safety, she wrapped her fingers tightly around the strange ring, spread her arms wide, closed her eyes…and jumped.

With a snort, she opened her eyes to see a large hairy spider about to crawl over her hand. With a faint whimper, she brushed it away into the dark corner of the shed and turned to leave, the ring lying unnoticed on the ground. Quickly, before the details began to fade, she ran up to her room and searched for the history of Hordrig Castle on her laptop. In amazement, she read an old article.

'Several accounts documented at the time confirm that Prince Ardan's soldiers watched the girl fall from the highest tower, yet a body was never found,' read Evie. *'She was later widely regarded to be a witch who had sprouted wings like the castle gargoyles and flown away to consort with her evil master.'*

Evie shook her head in amusement. If only they'd known the truth, it was far stranger. She was also pretty sure Daryn would have hated his description. Hoping that he had found happiness with Mila, she read on.

'The girl was believed to have conspired with Ethan, the Master Mason who confessed to exposing the Prince's secrets and stealing his treasure. Without trial, Ethan was condemned and beheaded for traitorous acts against the crown.'

An anguished cry escaped Evie, as she read the last line again. *He knew,* she thought to herself, remembering that look of sorrow on Ethan's face. *He knew what might happen and he still went ahead. I thought my task was to save him, not get him killed!* Heart sinking, and with scalding tears in her eyes, she forced herself to read on.

'What the Prince didn't know was that the Mason had not kept the treasure for himself, but instead had passed it on to the villagers in the lands around Ardan's castle. The desperate men used the treasure to fund an uprising against Prince Ardan – commonly recorded to be a cruel and vicious oppressor. After much fighting and loss of life on both sides, the Prince was eventually defeated, although his body was never recovered. A commoner, Will Drake, was elected to rule over the people of the region instead. Will governed peacefully and fairly for four decades before he succumbed to old age, leaving behind a legacy of hope and justice.'

With a sigh, Evie rested her tired head against the back of her chair. *The needs of the many outweigh the needs of the one*, she quoted. *He was a brave man indeed. But did I help to change history or just restore it?* she wondered, frowning in confusion, the possibilities scrambling her brain. *I'm really not sure I like this naquant business very much.* With a grimace she stood and closed the lid of her laptop, and sadly walked away.

…CONNECTING…

A n insistent rumble from her stomach reminded her she was still ravenous. She went down to the kitchen to make toast but hesitated as something niggled her. She frowned, then with sudden realisation bounded back to the shed.

The ring! I can't believe I forgot the ring. Did it even come back with me? Where is it?

Sighing in relief, she lifted it from the dark corner of the dusty floor. Once again, she felt the energy surge through her fingers and hastily put it in her pocket. She dashed back inside and up to Aaron's wardrobe. Hoisting the suitcase onto the bed, she opened the silk package, and lay the ring next to the other items.

Yes, they definitely belong together, I can feel the energy flow. But how do they connect? Maybe if I put this here, and that bit there…?

Growing excited, she slotted the pieces into position to form a device, using the flow of energy as a guide. The current grew stronger when the objects were in certain places but fell to low levels in others.

There, that must be it! The net is flowing through almost perfectly. She put down the device in satisfaction, then watched in dismay as the mechanism fell apart.

There must still be some pieces missing, maybe they won't lock together until everything is in place?

Frustrated, she packed everything away. Her instincts warned her it was critical she find the missing parts, time was running short.

Emil clenched his fists in irritation as the Vice Chancellor demanded his attention yet again. Smiling pleasantly, resisting the urge to snarl, he turned to look at the man. How he despised this weak, pathetic creature, always badgering him about recent decisions he had made as the Hantaiken Council Leader. His fingers itched to break his scrawny neck.

He recalled with pleasure the cruelties he had inflicted using the power of Prince Ardan, his favourite role until that wretched girl had interfered. After watching her jump from the tower, he'd questioned everyone in the castle about what had happened. He'd been rather surprised when the treacherous Mason had quietly confessed. Annoyance at his selfless bravery had made Emil act rashly, cutting off his head before he'd had chance to discover who had his treasure.

He'd been incensed when the uprising happened not long after, and even more surprised when he'd almost been captured after the final battle with the commoners. Only quick use of his el-VA had managed to spirit him away. He knew there would be no point returning to that timeline to undo the damage, he would never be able to change the minds of so many people – especially when they had the force of justice behind them.

He had neglected to tell Agathe any of this, of course, knowing his continued failures would cost him his life. Absently, he scratched at the healing scab around his eye. He needed to get enough authority to gain complete control of Hantaiken, even if that meant suffering these fawning fools. And he needed to return to Earth, he couldn't let Evie escape again. A shadow passed behind his eyes as he thought about the ways in which Agathe would make him regret his mistakes.

Finally, the meeting ended just as he reached the limit of his patience. Hurrying to his room, he locked the door and consulted his el-VA. There were no alerts that anyone had travelled to Hantaiken, but he knew it would only be a matter of time. It seemed Evie was destined to ruin all of his hard work. His life was difficult enough, keeping control of so many worlds while trying to avoid Agathe's frequent desires to hurt him.

Something close to panic quickened his breath as he planned his next steps. He decided to return to Earth, as he knew they must live in the general vicinity of that park, but his searches of the local registers had found no record of them. He assumed they were living under false names, so his only option was to search for them physically. Wearily, he sighed as he set the coordinates.

Emil strolled along the warm, sunny paths, monitoring his surroundings for any glimpse of the girl or that idiot Aaron. He was also on high alert for a glimpse of silvery hair, but failed to spot the bright, intelligent eyes watching him warily from deep within the bushes, stalking his every move.

Reaching the end of the park, he walked along the parade of shops and sat at a café table, so he could scrutinise the passersby. Sipping his lukewarm coffee, he glanced around, seemingly lost in thought but in reality carefully examining each face that walked past.

He had almost finished his cup when he noticed a commotion at the other end of the street. Quickly, he stood and strode towards the disturbance. As he did, he locked eyes with the red-faced man who was self-consciously trying to stuff his shopping back into a broken bag, obstructing the tide of impatient shoppers. Fierce joy curled Emil's upper lip and he broke into a run.

Aaron cursed his clumsiness yet again. Couldn't he go anywhere without tripping, dropping or breaking something? Embarrassed at the fuss he was causing, he crammed a tin of beans deeper into the already full bag and reached for the loose tomatoes rolling around. As he did, he happened to look up. Right into Emil's eyes, his handsome face twisted in malevolent triumph.

Aaron abandoned the bag and ran for his life, pushing past the startled onlookers. He knew he only had seconds before Emil's longer legs would catch up with him. And he wasn't sure he could beat him in a fair fight.

Coolly he assessed his options while he ran, in complete contrast to his usual awkwardness. He risked a quick glance behind and was relieved to see that Emil's progress was hampered by the busy afternoon crowd. He raced across the road and used the cover of a bus to slip into a narrow alleyway. Confident that Emil hadn't seen him, he sprinted to the end and followed the medieval passages to the large church. He planned to hide in there for a while until he could work out how to get both himself and Evie to safety.

Swiftly reaching the vast wooden doors, he paused at the sound of music playing and voices singing within. The choir was practicing for Sunday's evening service. Shrugging, he brushed wild curly hair from his face and went in anyway, quietly making his way up the steep, worn steps to the roof. Buffeted by the wind at this great height, Aaron leaned over the parapet to get a better view. The roads around were clear, there was no sign of Emil.

Gratefully, he leaned against the wall to catch his breath, hoping he had time to call Evie. Preoccupied by the search for his phone, which as ever eluded him, he whipped round in alarm as a familiar voice assailed him. Thinking quickly, he bent down to scoop something up, then turned to face Emil.

'You can't escape this time, Aaron. I have you now. And once I've finished with you, I'll deal with Evie.' Emil cackled, his laughter laced with a note of hysteria at finally catching his prey.

'How on earth did you know where I'd gone?' asked Aaron, baffled.

'You're too easy to predict,' taunted Emil. 'You seem to forget that we trained together, learned tactics together, fought together. I knew you'd go to a high point to assess the situation, this was the natural choice.'

Aaron kicked himself for being so obvious. He assumed an attack position.

'Well come on then, let's get it over with,' he sighed.

Emil sprang at him, but was stunned by the brick that Aaron threw at him. He staggered, blood dripping into his eyes from the deep cut in his forehead, helpless for a moment while Aaron disappeared down the stairs. Shaking his head to clear his vision, smearing blood across his face, he stumbled after him, feeling the dark anger inside beginning to unfold.

Aaron pelted down the stairs, along the aisle and into the gloomy cloisters. Barely pausing to let his eyes adjust to the deepening shadows, he ran to the other end to find the exit. Panting for breath, he cursed at the locked door. Heavy footsteps echoed in the passage behind him and he turned to defend against Emil, who had flung himself at him.

They crashed to the floor in a tangle of limbs and groans of pain, but quickly moved apart to gain an advantage. Circling warily, Emil moved suddenly to the left. Aaron ignored the feint and instead came straight at him, elbow raised to strike at his face. Emil ducked and his momentum carried them both towards the cloister wall. They crashed heavily into the unyielding stone, the noise masked by the soaring notes of the choir. Emil's bulk knocked the wind out of Aaron. Sensing his dominance, Emil brought his knee up to finish the job.

Before he could connect with Aaron's unprotected face, he was knocked off target by a smaller, solid weight as Finn threw himself at Emil. Landing on his chest, he brandished a sharp knife at Emil's exposed neck, then sunk it deep into the meaty flesh around the shoulder blade. Emil roared in pain and backhanded the boy across the cold stone floor, where he lay stunned.

Seizing his chance, Aaron picked up a flowerpot from the nearby sill and smashed it down on Emil's head as he struggled to get up, the small dagger still imbedded in his shoulder. The big man slumped, unconscious, and Aaron hurried over to the dazed boy lying on the floor.

'There now, lad,' he said, helping him to slowly sit up. 'Let's both get out of here before he wakes up. He'll be doubly dangerous now he's wounded, he'll tear the town apart to find us. I need to get Evie to safety, and quickly. She needs to know how much danger we're in.'

The boy stood, leaning on Aaron for support, and

together they emerged from the church. Resting for a moment, blinking in the setting sun, the boy looked at Aaron.

'My name is Finn,' he said quietly. 'The net sent me here. Take care of Evie, don't let Emil get her. Her fate hangs in the balance.'

With that, eyes shadowed by dark thoughts, Finn disappeared into the quantum network.

Aaron hurried home, concerned for Evie's safety. He burst into the kitchen, calling out her name.

'Aaron, what on earth's the matter,' she cried, running down the stairs at the panic in his voice.

'Emil has found us, we need to get moving,' he warned, hugging her tightly. 'We're both in trouble if he gets his hands on us.'

She pushed away from him and looked up into his face, open-mouthed. 'Emil? How can you possibly know who he is, you didn't travel with me? Aaron, what is going on?'

She glared at him, hands on hips.

Confusion played across his face, cleared by a sudden realisation.

'Oh Evie, you've discovered the net? Why didn't you tell me? No wonder you've been looking so worried recently.'

He framed her face with his hands and tenderly brushed a lock of hair away from her tired face. Taking a deep breath to steady himself, he gestured to the table.

'Sit down,' he ordered. 'It's about time I told you

everything. But first, tell me what has happened to you, it's important that I hear all of it.'

Slowly, Evie sank into the chair, reeling from the fact that Aaron seemed to know all about the net. She took a moment to gather her scattered thoughts, and began to relate recent events.

'And that's about it,' she finished, exhausted after the long tale. 'Basically, I'm a naquant who seems to be undoing damage caused by Emil's meddling. He's already killed Anya, he *really* wants to kill me, Finn is protecting me, and I can't shake the feeling that Mom is still alive.'

She slumped forward and laid her hands on her arms, looking sideways at him through half-closed lids.

He sat, shaken by her last words. He had no naquant ability himself, so could never sense Ellen's lifeforce. But had enough experience to know that a powerful naquant might be able to detect the energy of other naquants, no matter how far away. He looked at Evie with renewed respect, and hope.

'You've had to deal with so much. I only wish you could have told me sooner.'

'I assumed you'd think I was crazy if I started telling you all this,' she replied. 'Life hasn't exactly been normal recently, how was I to know you'd believe me so easily? I think it's time for your side of the story, Aaron.'

She straightened and waited expectantly. Aaron licked his lips, wondering where to begin.

'I trained with Emil on Eigenstat, where OPOL has its headquarters,' he said at last. 'We were both agents of OPOL, which by then was being run by Agathe, the genius behind lifoNET. She is one ruthless woman, Evie, I hope you don't ever get to meet her.'

He walked to the kettle and flicked it on, knowing a hot cup of tea would help them cope.

'We learned how to use the net. Not using our own abilities, of course, as few agents had any by then. We need an el-VA to travel. It allows us to do almost everything you can, but can create a channel anywhere, any time.'

Pulling a device out of his pocket, he tossed it to her while he poured water into the cups. She looked at it curiously, sensing that part of the device extended into the net, crossing the divide between planes of existence. She stroked her fingers across the length of the el-VA, lost in thought.

'Don't touch any of the buttons,' he warned. 'It's been deactivated, but who knows what a naquant could do with it. I can't come after you if you accidentally reactivate it.'

Evie hastily pushed it away from her.

He handed her a cup of tea, clumsily tipping a few scalding drops onto her fingers. She winced, then sipped cautiously.

Warming to his subject, he continued. 'We were sent to various places, to convince specific people to do certain things. At first, I thought it was kind of fun, no harm in it. It wasn't like I was telling people to go to war, or anything.'

He stopped, then looked down at his hands, fingers

anxiously entwined. 'Then I decided to return to one of the worlds. I'd fallen for a local girl, you see, despite repeated warnings during our training not to get involved. When I got there, I found out she was dead.'

He looked up into Evie's questioning eyes. 'My task had been to persuade her father, the city blacksmith, to trade with a rival town. I didn't see any harm in it, helping him to expand his business and all that.'

Grimacing, he continued bitterly. 'I was young and I was stupid, and that blinded me to the fact that such an act might be regarded as treason, trading weapons with the enemy. Oh, Agathe knew exactly what she was doing when she sent me. The blacksmith was strung up from the walls as a warning, his family was driven into the wilderness. They were set upon by bandits, of course. All of them killed without mercy for their pitiful belongings.'

He put his face in his hands, and Evie slipped her arm around his shoulders.

'The suspicion caused by the blacksmith's 'treachery' made the two cities eventually come to blows,' he said, the words muffled through his fingers. 'Both were ransacked, houses destroyed, lots of people died. And all because of one seemingly innocent choice, suggested by me.'

Slamming his fist onto the table, making her jump and the tea slosh, he cursed angrily.

'I vowed then I would never do Agathe's bidding again. I went back to lifoNET and confronted her, demanded to know what she was playing at. I even told her I quit.'

Puzzled, he said, 'For some reason, though, she wasn't angry. Just disappointed, as though I'd offended her somehow. I'd expected much more, knowing her reputation. Instead, she almost begged me to do one last job for her, one of protection this time. Well, I couldn't really refuse.'

Taking Evie's face into his hands, he smiled gently at her. 'Agathe sent me to watch over you and Ellen. Your mother used to work for OPOL as well, you know.'

He laughed at her shocked face.

'Naquants were disappearing fast, and she wanted to keep an eye on you both. When Ellen left the agency to have you, Agathe still wanted her naquant abilities. She wanted *you* because of your potential. Your father was also a naquant, and an OPOL agent alongside your mother. A very rare partnership existed between them, which means you are very special indeed.'

Evie sank into the chair, overwhelmed by the revelations. 'Why are we on the run then, if Agathe sent you to protect us? Why is Emil trying to kill me?'

'Oh, he's not trying to kill you. He wants to capture you for Agathe. You see, it turns out that Agathe didn't really want to protect you after all. No, she desperately wanted what Liam had stolen from her.'

He stood up and led her towards the stairs.

'He had realised long before anyone else that Agathe needed to be stopped. So he stole the master plans to lifoNET. With those, anyone could destroy it and end Agathe's ability to influence other worlds. He hid the plans, left clues to their location that could only be found by other naquants, then disappeared. No-one has heard from him since.'

Flinging open his wardrobe, he pulled out the suitcase.

'Agathe was furious, of course. I'm guessing that's why so many naquants have gone missing, she's probably been interrogating them. She used me to monitor Ellen, who had been closest to Liam. Knowing me well, she assumed I would gain Ellen's affection and trust, and learn where the plans were being kept. Then I could report back to Agathe. Always deviously plotting, that woman – there is no end to her scheming.'

He unwrapped the silk scarf and turned to watch Evie's reaction. She looked at him sheepishly, her cheeks burning.

'Actually, I knew they were here. I sort of discovered them a while ago.'

Aaron raised his eyebrows at her prying, while she quickly showed him how they connected.

'The net flows, but everything falls apart when I let go. There is something missing, but how can we ever find it?'

Aaron picked up the ring. 'Where did this come from, it's not one of Ellen's?'

'I discovered it, hidden in a bag of treasure. I could feel the energy flowing from it, a kind of tingle. The same feeling that I had when I held the other items.'

He looked at her in surprise. 'A tingle? Hmmm…I don't feel anything. Maybe that's how Ellen discovered the others, the net led her to the right location? I can't think of any other reason why you'd be there at the exact place and time to find this specific ring.'

He stood decisively. 'You are in grave danger, Evie. You don't have the training to control your abilities, yet I have no doubt you will be travelling again. I can't protect you when you go, not without an active el-VA. But I can give you something to defend yourself with.'

Turning back to the wardrobe, he wormed his way in to collect a metal box. Unlocking it with a small key hung around his neck, he pulled out an object shaped like a computer mouse.

'Give me your hand,' he ordered. Placing her first two fingers onto the indentations on the top of the device and her thumb into one on the side, he turned it over and pressed certain symbols imprinted underneath.

'There, now it's keyed to your fingerprints, no-one else can use it. It's a neural disruptor, designed by Agathe so it can travel the net. Press that button there for a wide beam, this one for a narrow beam. The slider changes its intensity. You can't kill anyone with it, but you can choose to stun them or knock them out completely. Keep it safe at all times, you might need it.'

Evie warily zipped it into a trouser pocket.

Frowning, she blurted out, 'Aaron, are you still reporting to Agathe?'

'What? No, of course not. Agathe was right, of course, I did fall in love with your mother. I couldn't lie to her though, I told Ellen the truth. We decided I should keep up the pretence of being an OPOL agent, to keep you safe. That all changed the day they killed her.'

He stopped and looked at her, unsure how she'd react to the news.

'Agathe killed my mother. Are you sure?' Evie licked her lips and frowned as he shrugged.

'I assumed so, although now I'm not so certain. Maybe they took her elsewhere, a body was never found after all. Just like when your father disappeared, or so I was told. Have you really been dreaming about her?'

'Yes, but I don't think they're just dreams, they're too intense. If she is trapped somewhere, we need to find her! If my dreams are right, she is all alone. Aaron, I can't bear the thought.'

Evie threw herself onto the bed and wept. He sat next to her, soothingly rubbing her back until the flood of emotion had passed. Handing her a tissue, he walked to the window while she composed herself.

'Now Emil knows we're here, he'll stop at nothing to find us. He seemed rather stressed when I saw him, which makes him even more dangerous than normal. I only managed to escape this time because Finn helped me. The boy seemed to know you, Evie?'

'He does, he's saved my life twice now! I do hope I get chance to thank him one day,' she replied, the thought of the silver-haired boy sending a non-naquant tingle down her spine.

'What are we going to do, Aaron? I'm scared.'

He sat next to her, pulling her close. 'We need to leave, today. I have a safe place we can go to. We need to find what else Liam might have hidden before Agathe does. We have to shut down lifoNET and stop Agathe – before you get hurt and she becomes too powerful.'

He smiled tentatively. 'We have a lot of work ahead. But we'll be stronger together. We are never truly alone, you know, we're all connected whether we realise it or not. Everything is woven into the fabric of life.'

Evie took his hand and squeezed tightly, relieved she didn't have to face this alone.

4. YOU WILL OBEY

'We know that no one ever seizes power with the intention of relinquishing it.'

—*George Orwell*

S he hadn't enjoyed hastily packing her bags and fleeing their comfortable life with Aaron. Hours of travelling in a hot car had taken them to a small, dark cottage on an exposed clifftop. The summer winds whistled around numerous nooks and crannies, sending mournful notes through her nightly terrors. They had only been there a couple of days and already she wanted to go home.

'I'm sorry Evie, but it is safer here for now. If you don't travel, that is. lifoNET is no doubt tracing any surges you might make. We'll have to manage until I can work out what to do next.'

With that, Aaron had given her a distracted pat and wandered off into the kitchen garden.

Evie sat on her bed and unwrapped the items yet again, pressing the silky scarf against her face and wetting it with her tears. She cursed loudly as the ring, hidden in the folds, slid free and bounced on the wooden floorboards, disappearing under the bed. Sighing, she crawled into the dark and dusty depths, trying to feel around and avoid any spiderwebs. After a moment, it occurred to her that the bed couldn't be this wide. She looked back to see a faint glimmer of light from her room, then become dizzy as she felt her mind *dissolve* through the floor and into the net.

She landed on a small, prickly bush, sharp spikes grazing her skin. Wincing in pain, she climbed out onto the worn road and immediately began shivering. Her thin clothes were no match for the freezing, snow-laden wind that howled around her body, and she knew she would have to reach shelter quickly.

She decided to check the net, to see if it would help her decide which direction to take. Closing her eyes, she concentrated hard, her mind sensing the strands *underneath* reality. Much of the net in this world was broken and distorted, but two clear directions were apparent. One led back into the lonely wilderness, but her cold body rejected that option. The other led towards a city, which she could just see in the far distance. Anticipating the warmth and shelter she would find there, she strode off in that direction, head down, vigorously rubbing her cold, sore arms.

Clearly, she had misjudged how far away she was because the city didn't seem to be getting any nearer and she was reaching the end of her strength. Shivering and exhausted, she trudged along, wondering why she had landed in this miserable place. Shuddering violently, she stumbled and fell into the soft, embracing snow.

So, this is it, she thought dreamily. *After everything I've been through, I freeze to death. Can you travel if you're frozen in place? I'm not sure Aaron could cope if I don't return, he's not exactly practical. He'll probably burn the house down. That's if Emil doesn't get him first!* She tried to fight the relentless lethargy, desperately wanting to go back home. But instead she sighed, her breath freezing in the icy air. Lacking the energy to fight back, she closed her eyes and resigned herself to certain death.

It came as rather a surprise when gentle hands lifted her up and bundled her into a warm, fluffy blanket.

'This is what happens when you live as a Wilder,' scolded a low, but feminine voice. 'You wander off, freeze solid, and no-one knows about it until the ice thaws. Why you are so against technology and implants, I'll never know.'

The woman hesitated as she looked more closely at Evie's face.

'How strange,' she murmured. 'You look very much like someone I used to know." She frowned, shook her head slightly, then wrapped the blanket tighter around the shivering girl.

Evie opened her eyes and watched as the tall, young-looking woman tutted and placed her into a vehicle that was hovering above the ground. Amazed at the sight, and wanting to question the woman further, Evie struggled to stay awake. But, accompanied by the soothing sound of air whooshing by as they travelled over the land, she drifted off, her senses tingling as she watched the swing of a heavy pendant at the woman's throat, a large blue gem trapped in delicate grey filigree.

Before long, Evie felt the hover slow down. She sleepily opened her eyes, then sat up in shock at the sight of the city. The white buildings must have been covered by a transparent energy shield; while the hover was covered in a thick layer of snow, the heavy blizzard could not penetrate and instead melted on contact, cascading down like a waterfall dome.

Evie watched as the woman leaned closer to the entrance and her head was scanned. 'Ariadne Collings/unknown female child' flashed above the opening that appeared and they manoeuvred through, snow swirling under the hover as they entered. The heat of the city washed over her, and she threw off her blanket. Stretching in the pleasant air, she turned to her companion.

'Thanks for rescuing me. Where are we going?'

'Hmm, you really are a Wilder,' replied Ariadne. 'Otherwise your implant would tell you where we are going. This is Hantaiken, of course. What is your name, young lady? And how did you get separated from your family?'

Evie hesitated, unsure whether she could trust this stern

woman. 'I'm Evie. I got lost in the blizzard. I don't have a family, my mother died when I was young.' Her evident sadness caused Ariadne's eyes to soften.

She stroked Evie's hair. 'I am sorry my child, you are so young to be alone. If you agree, I will take you home with me until we can decide what to do with you. I warn you though, I may have to take you to the Council.'

Alarmed by this prospect, Evie sat back to look around, anxious to change the subject.

'What is wrong with those people?' she asked, gawping at the silent, orderly crowd that followed unseen lines on the pavement. 'They aren't robots, are they?'

'Don't be silly, girl. They are simply following the path to their designated destination. Please tell me you've at least visited Hantaiken before?'

Evie slowly shook her head. Exasperated, Ariadne said, 'All city dwellers are implanted as soon as they are born, and live their lives connected to the net. The net teaches us everything we need to know, and we have entertainment whenever we think about it. When we are grown, it decides what our occupation will be, according to any particular skills we might have, and assigns us to the relevant work and rest roster. We are also matched to a life mate, based on our personalities and interests. We are never alone; at any time, we can contact anybody in the city. For a city dweller to be disconnected is like a death sentence. The loneliness would no doubt kill us.'

Evie was repulsed by the idea. She loved being with other

people but needed to spend time alone. The thought of no real privacy horrified her. 'You won't make me have the implant, will you?' she asked worriedly.

'I will try my best, if that's what you want,' replied the woman. 'But if you decide against it, you will need to return to the wild. You wouldn't be able to live here, you would never belong. No need to worry about that just yet though, we will go to my home first and rest.'

A thought struck Evie. 'Why were you out in the wild, if being disconnected from the net means death? You seem pretty lively to me?'

The woman glanced at her. 'Some of us can stand being alone for a short time, it seems. I discovered my ability a few years ago, when my implant failed. At first, it felt like I'd gone blind *and* deaf. The solitude almost drove me crazy. Instead, I thought back to what life had been like before I was sent here, living without an implant. I was about the age you are now, I guess, so I remembered. Even so, I babbled almost non-stop to the technicians until they repaired me. From that day onwards, probably because it was clear that I could cope, I was reassigned to the scouting team and regularly go out to find new food sources and trade with the local Wilders.' She hesitated, then whispered, 'Don't tell anyone, but I actually enjoy the time alone now. I have room to think. I expect you know what I mean, as you're not connected.'

Evie nodded in agreement. 'I might not be connected to the net, but I'm starting to realise that everyone is connected, none of us are truly alone – Life joins us together.' She paused, not wanting to offend Ariadne, but continued, 'And without an implant, we are free to choose the life we want to lead, we aren't told what to do by a string of algorithms.'

Ariadne smiled at the thought. 'What a thing to believe. I didn't realise Wilders were in any way spiritual, I thought they were just…well, wild! You'll have to tell me more.' She turned back to the road ahead.

Just then, a black hover came speeding towards them, the silent city dwellers standing back in unison to let it pass. A loud, metallic voice boomed, 'Halt, exit the vehicle slowly! Halt, exit the vehicle slowly!' Ariadne looked at Evie in bewilderment, wondering why her implant was not providing any information. She stopped and gestured for Evie to climb down.

As soon as her feet hit the ground, Evie was grabbed by a large, faceless robot that flung her onto its back seat and closed the thick, transparent lid. Hearing the lock clunk, she yelled to be let out, banging her fists against the strengthened glass.

Glimpsing Evie's white face but unable to reach her in time, Ariadne could only watch as the hover disappeared into the distance.

Evie fumed when the robot refused to even acknowledge her, let alone answer any questions. Helpless to act, she slumped in the hard seat and seethed. Gazing out the window to distract herself, she shivered as she watched the

Hantaikens walking along almost in step, eerily quiet as they focused on their internal monitors. Part of her recognised their vacant, disconnected stare, uncomfortably like her own when she was absorbed by her phone.

She had just promised herself that she would never become that bad when the hover descended into a tunnel near the heart of the city. She sat up eagerly, keen to see where she was being taken. But one featureless subterranean passageway followed another, each safeguarded by a security barrier, and she sank back, hungry and bored. *We must be outside the city limits again, we've travelled so far.*

Eventually, they arrived at a large, solid gate and came to a stop. 'Disembark,' the robot commanded, releasing the lock on her door.

She climbed out, glad to stretch her legs. To one side of the gate, she noticed a small, unobtrusive sign. *'DysGen Facility' – I wonder what that means?* she thought, then glared at the robot as it shoved her through the gate that was sliding open.

Inside was as grey as the rock outside, but the corridor was smooth metal. She plodded through, exhaustion slowing her steps. After yet more security scans, they finally arrived in a large common room. A dozen pairs of curious eyes watched as the robot propelled her along and into a tiny, utilitarian bedroom. Turning back to protest, she had a moment to note that they were all children like her, before the metal door trundled down, locking her in.

She sat on the hard bed and began to wait impatiently,

drumming her fingers on the metal table bolted to the wall. After a while, she climbed to her feet and stalked around the room, the lack of a window and confined space making her claustrophobic. Realising that she wasn't going to be let out anytime soon, she lay down to rest. Drained, it didn't take long for her eyes to grow heavy, and she fell deeply asleep.

Evie ran through a shadowy landscape, the dark road stretching out before her, sharp stones lacerating her feet. *I'm coming, Mom, wait for me*, she whimpered, slipping in the trickling blood. The distant shrieks began to weaken and she stumbled, heartsick at the desolation in the cries. As an incandescent streak lit the surrounding gloom, she caught a glimpse of what lay ahead. Evie began to scream.

A loud bell jolted her awake and she sat up, drenched in sweat. She took a few deep breaths to steady herself, trying to shake the remnants of the nightmare. Groggily, she rubbed her eyes and yawned, startled when the door suddenly rolled up. A delightful aroma made her stomach growl and she decided to follow her nose.

Silence fell as she wandered into the common room, and she froze uncertainly. Regaining her composure, she calmly walked over to the food counter, took a plate of…whatever that was, and sat down. Slowly, the chatter grew louder, and a group of children came to sit beside her.

'So, when did your implant 'fail' then?' demanded a tall dark-haired boy, stealing some food from her plate.

'Oi! Cheeky…,' smiled Evie. She hesitated, wondering whether she should tell them the truth. 'I don't have an implant,' she said at last.

The others stared at her in shock. 'But you can't be a Wilder,' exclaimed the dark, curly-haired girl to her left. 'You're too clean, and those clothes never came from an animal.' She plucked at Evie's t-shirt.

'You're right, I'm not a Wilder either. I'm not even from this planet. I have this ability to travel between worlds, through the net – the Quantum Universal Network that connects everything. I've haven't done it very often though.' She looked up and chuckled at the faces staring at her in mixed wonder and disbelief.

'You're having us on!' cried the boy, becoming angry.

'Not at all, I'm telling you the truth. But I'm not sure what to do next. I know I must be here for a reason, but so far I have no idea what's going on.'

'Well, you're talking to the right person,' declared the boy self-importantly. 'My name's Xandro, Xan to my friends, and my father is the Vice Chancellor. But I've had enough of my implant, I can tell you. Always being told what to do and when to do it, it's boring! I've been disobeying my instructions for a long time, sneaking off whenever I could. I didn't think anyone had noticed. I want to become a Wilder and be free. That's probably why you're here, to help me.'

'Xan, I can't imagine being a Wilder is much fun either.

Ariadne said that Wilders were against technology. That means they must do everything for themselves. Grow food, raise livestock, clean everything by hand, make clothes – it's incredibly hard work! No time for fun and entertainment, that's for sure. Do you think you could cope with that?'

The children looked at each other, dismayed at the thought.

'I could try,' said Xan, determined. 'I really can't stand being ordered around anymore, it's like an itch in my head that I can't get rid of.' The others nodded in agreement.

'Is that why you're here?' asked Evie. 'Did you come here by yourself, to get rid of your implant?'

Xan looked at his friends. 'No, not really. One day, I couldn't access my implant anymore, it was like a blank wall in my mind. I started to panic, who could I tell? We're not supposed to be able to disobey our implants, and I'm guessing mine had failed for some reason. But I didn't have to worry for too long, as I was collected by the RoboPol very quickly.'

He sank into his seat, despondent. 'I didn't even have chance to say goodbye to my family. I've asked around and everyone has had a similar experience. I know people have been disappearing recently, but nobody knows what happened to them. Maybe they were collected like us, maybe our implants are going to be repaired? We've been here for days already, but no-one has told us why we're here or what's going to happen to us.' He stopped, the last remnants of bravado vanishing in the face of reality. 'I was hoping they would at least release us to the Wilders, but now I'm not so sure.'

Evie put a comforting arm around his shoulders. 'Don't worry,' she said, turning back to her plate to shovel food into her mouth. 'We'll think of something. The RoboPol probably brought me here because I don't even have an implant, so perhaps they will take us all to the Wilders. That must be it, because I am almost certain we're not in the city anymore. I wonder if we can find someone to ask?'

As she spoke, there was a commotion at the other end of the room. They stood to get a better look as a RoboPol squad marched in, led by a large, powerful man. His face was shadowed by the powerful spotlight behind him, but Evie stared at him, her heart racing. *It…it can't be him? Please don't let it be him.* As he turned to face the room, fear washed over her and she shrank back, the strange food churning uneasily in her stomach. His eyes swept the room, searching, and she crouched down even further behind a chair. Frowning, rubbing a healing scab around one eye, he ordered half the children to line up. They quickly obeyed under his intense glare.

'Move,' he barked, pointing at the open door, and they quietly filed out.

Evie released the breath she'd been holding, her fingers trembling as she wondered what on earth she was going to do now. Emil was here, and clearly in charge. She desperately wanted to leave but was trapped. She had no idea how to use her abilities to get back home and the knowledge terrified her. She thought longingly of the disrupter she had forgotten, still packed in her suitcase.

Taking a deep breath to steady herself, gathering her courage, she stood up and began mingling with those who remained, determined to discover what was going on and, more importantly, whether she could do anything about it.

Evie frowned, trying to work it all out. It seemed that Emil was known as Yannis on this world, the leader of the Council. He had been in Hantaiken for a long time, well liked and respected. Using his charm and influence, he had taken control of the Council five cycles ago.

Since then, life had become more regulated and demanding for everyone, a change that had surprised all those who had voted for the big, seemingly easy-going man. There was no longer any free time, and everyone had to complete their work schedule or face losing their food allowance – or worse, if the rumours were true.

'In fact,' Xan had confided, 'I am not sure how I got away with it for so long! I suspect my father may have been covering for me. And now I have ended up here and shamed him.' He walked away, troubled.

Most of the children had similar stories, confirming Evie's gut feeling that Emil was once again up to no good. She nibbled her nails, wondering what she could do. She was only a child; how could she ever stand up to the powerful leader of a city? Despite their short acquaintance, she really wished Ariadne was here to help her again.

She looked up as the exit door slid open and jumped to her feet, debating whether she could make a run for it. As she hesitated, another door leading deeper into the facility rose up. Out streamed the group of children that had been taken earlier, heads down, walking in time.

Xan rushed up to a friend, crying out her name. 'Sally, Sally, are you ok? Sally, it's me, Xan. What's the matter with you? Sally!' He stopped and stood mutely, watching as she meekly followed the others without saying a word or even looking at him. 'Sally?' he murmured softly to her retreating back. The final child left the facility and the exit door slammed shut once more.

Evie grabbed Xan and whispered in his ear. 'She had no idea who you were, she didn't even hear you. It was almost as though she was being controlled.'

She gasped as she realised the likely truth. 'That's probably what *has* happened, they have been brain wiped and the implant restored! They must want to do the same to you. I don't have an implant, but I'm sure Emi...Yannis has other plans for me. We've got to get out of here,' she said, desperately.

To her horror, Emil abruptly loomed in the still open doorway. Their eyes met and his face lit up exultantly.

'That surge was you after all,' he gloated. 'I was right to pick you up.'

'Get her,' he ordered, and Evie screamed as a RoboPol glided over to grab her by the arms.

'Xan, help me,' she cried, as it lifted her up and moved towards the door. But he could only watch helplessly as they quickly disappeared into the brightly lit tunnel.

Emil strode down one hallway after another, the RoboPol easily keeping pace and holding Evie tightly in its pincers despite her frantic kicks. Suddenly he halted and entered a code into a metal door. Standing aside as the door slid open, he gestured for her to enter, inclining his head in mock courtesy.

Evie scowled as she was carried unwillingly into the large laboratory. She began struggling again, fear turning her insides to liquid.

'Don't kill me, I don't want to die,' she shouted, her arms bruising as she tried to wriggle free.

'I'm not going to kill you, girl, despite all the trouble you've caused me. No, you're far too valuable for that. Besides, Agathe would watch me die slowly and very painfully if you were harmed before she had chance to use you. That's who you should be worried about, not me.'

Evie paled and drooped in the robot's grip. 'Why can't you all leave me alone, I just want a normal life.'

'You're not normal though, Evie, that's the problem. Agathe wants you and she won't stop until she gets you.'

He bent over a bed and loosened some straps. 'Now, be a good girl and lie down so we can strap you in.'

The RoboPol lifted her onto the bed and Emil tightened

the straps across her ankles and wrists. Tears streaked their way down Evie's face.

'Oh, don't cry. You remind me too much of your mother when you do that.'

'My mother? She's dead, what do you know about her?'

'Oh, I knew her well. She was once very close and dear to me. Even *I* was sorry to see how she ended up. But, hey ho, life goes on. There are more important things to consider now. I need to send you to Agathe, and quickly. My life depends on it.'

'I have no idea what you're talking about, you're scaring me,' whispered Evie.

Emil laughed, enjoying her distress. 'Not as much as Agathe will. You'll need this injection when you get there, believe me. Lie still, or it will hurt even more.'

Evie stiffened, then began thrashing wildly. 'Help, please help me!' she shouted, knowing it was pointless, she was on her own.

She gaped in astonishment when Ariadne came bursting into the room, disabling the RoboPol with a blast of energy. Emil swung round at the noise, hesitating when he saw her disruptor. Recovering quickly, he leapt at her, covering the distance in moments. Ariadne had just enough time to direct the ray towards him, and he fell heavily to the floor, deeply stunned. Turning him over, grunting at the weight, Ariadne tied his wrists tightly behind him and turned to Evie.

'Hurry, we don't have much time,' she said, releasing Evie from the straps, who groaned as she sat up, rubbing her wrists.

'I reprogrammed the RoboPol to go into the city, but they'll be returning soon. And this creature won't be out of action for much longer. We really don't want to be around when he wakes up.'

She grabbed Evie and pulled her towards the door. 'Come on, let's go. Follow me, we'll collect the others on our way. We must flee to the Wilders, they're our only sanctuary now.'

Sometime later, Evie was struggling to catch her breath as she sprinted alongside the other children, feet sinking into the deep snow.

'How did you find us?' she wondered. 'I didn't think anyone would know where we were, so deep underground.'

'I'm a scout, remember. We are given certain access codes, so we can get out of the city. We also have much more freedom than normal citizens, so I don't have to account for all of my movements. *And* I must turn my implant off whenever I leave Hantaiken. All of these factors have been most useful recently.'

She held up her hand to stop the group, bending over to recover her breath.

'I'd started to investigate as soon as I heard that people were disappearing. I'm good with technology, so I hacked my way into the net, gave myself superuser access and permission to enter any part of the city. DysGen has cropped up quite a few times while I've been poking around. It's certainly associated with an unusual amount of RoboPol activity. I decided to find out where they were based.' She paused and looked up at Evie.

'I don't like mysteries, I like answers. Your face reminds me of someone I used to know, which is impossible, and you were whisked off without any of the normal warnings we would get through our implant. I needed to find out more.'

She stood and waved everybody on with a weary warning that they still had a long way to go.

'So how did you find me?' asked Evie, struggling to keep up with the woman's long stride.

'I accessed the net to see where they were taking you. But there was nothing in the public domain, which is unusual as all citizens are informed if there is unrest. In your case, there was no news at all. When I dug a little deeper, I *did* find a high-security, top-secret command hiding behind a certain RoboPol's programming. It led me straight to you in the laboratory at DysGen.'

Taking Evie's small cold hand and rubbing gently to warm it, she asked, 'Why are they so interested in you?'

'I don't know, really I don't,' said Evie. 'Emil thought I was important for some reason, but apart from being able to travel the net, I am no-one special.'

'Emil? You mean Yannis? He told you his real name?' exclaimed Ariadne. 'And you can travel the net without help?' She exhaled slowly. 'A naquant! No wonder he was after you, there are only a handful of you left. We must protect you at all costs.'

'That still doesn't explain why I'm on this world,' said

Evie, frustrated. 'Why would the net send me here?'

'To undo the damage OPOL has caused?' ventured Ariadne. 'If you succeed and Agathe fails, she won't try again. It takes massive amounts of energy to power lifoNET, so she has no choice but to focus the energy elsewhere instead. Actually, no-one is quite sure how Agathe powers the machine.'

She broke off as they heard movement in front of them. And behind them. And to the side. Ariadne whipped out her stunner, but a deep, gruff voice cut her short.

'I wouldn't if I were you, girlie. We might only have crossbows, but there are ten of them trained on you right now, and they won't miss if you fire that gun. Put it on the floor…slowly.'

Ariadne bent down to comply.

'All of you, put your hands on your heads and walk forward. No sudden moves please, we don't want any unfortunate accidents.'

They began walking, Evie looking everywhere to find the source of the voice. She couldn't see anyone hiding in the snow-laden trees. Just as the last of them passed the fallen stunner, a small, wiry man jumped out of the foliage and picked it up, looking at it with disdain. Several other men and women revealed themselves, the crossbows never wavering as they approached the group. An older man stepped forward, his long hair and beard dusted with grey.

'Santos,' exclaimed Ariadne. 'It's me, Ari. Thank goodness, I was coming to find you. We need a safe place to hide, and I trust you. Will you help us?'

'Ari? Ari, it *is* you! Come here and give old Santos a hug. What are you doing so far from home? And who are all these children? They look like city dwellers to me.' He sighed. 'There's going to be trouble ahead, isn't there? I can feel it in my bones, this isn't good news. Come, let's find a safe, warm place first, and you can tell me more. Children, are you up for a little hike? It won't be far, I promise.'

'"Won't be far",' grumbled Xan to Evie, his feet throbbing. '"Little hike", he said. He's a worse slave driver than the net! We've been walking for hours and hours.'

Evie didn't reply, wearily flapping her hand at him. She plodded on, not sure if she could travel much further. The visit to this world was lasting much longer than the others, and she was worried she might never get home. Just as she thought she couldn't walk another step, Santos raised his arm and pointed towards a cave, the entrance partially hidden by hanging vines.

'In there, come on now. Food, drink and sleep awaits. And answers, I hope.' He ushered them inside. Evie stumbled through the gap, the warmth and noise in the massive cave hitting her like a wall. She found a space to rest and collapsed in a wet heap, Xan still beside her.

They both watched tiredly as the Wilders went about their familiar tasks, wool-clad bodies busily moving around while they organized supper. The fire was already crackling and popping when they arrived, but the meat had to be prepared, the vegetables cleaned and cut, the water put on to boil. And then the interminable wait while the stew cooked. The delicious aromas filled the cavernous space, making her stomach rumble.

Xan moaned, 'A quick press of a few buttons, that's all I do at home. Anything from the menu, just like that! I *suppose* I could get used to all this waiting around, in time. But it does look like hard work.'

Evie bit her lip to stop the sharp words she was longing to say. He was complaining after one meal, which he didn't even have to cook himself! She had a feeling he wasn't really cut out for the Wilder life.

Bored of sitting still for so long, she stood up and tried to spot Ariadne. She saw her at the back of the cave, talking earnestly to Santos, and decided to join them. She needed answers, or she would be stuck here forever.

'Evie!' Ariadne greeted her as she walked over, Xan traipsing after her. 'I was just telling Santos about you. Considering your evident importance, he is worried that Yannis will come after you. And he thinks that letting you stay here could put all of his Wilders in danger.'

'I'm a nobody though! I have no idea why he wants me, and I don't care. I travelled the net for a reason and I need to find out what that is. As soon as that's sorted, I'll be able to go home, and you'll be safe.'

'I am not sure safety exists these days anyway,' replied Santos, his face creased in worry. 'My people are finding it harder and harder to find food, most of it is being *requisitioned* by Hantaiken. And we need to travel further afield each day just to find enough resources to make clothes or tools. My heart is heavy saying this, but we may have to join the city and become implanted, probably sooner rather than later. Or we will dwindle and die. I will *not* let that be the fate of my people.'

Ariadne looked at him in shock. 'You can't let that happen!' she cried. '*We* can't let that happen. My time as a scout has given me a much better understanding of the Wilders. Your life isn't perfect, by any means, but you have a freedom that is priceless. Hantaiken has lost that freedom, and we didn't even notice until it was too late.'

Evie's skin prickled as she began to realise why she might be here. She was the catalyst that had brought these people together. Santos was the leader of his people, Ariadne was…well, more important than a mere scout, of that she was certain. And Xan's father had the ear of the council, with Xan likely to follow in his footsteps when he was older. All of them were in a position to *do* something, to change their lives for the better. It would take courage, but it was clear they already had that in abundance. Tentatively, she stepped forward and began to speak.

'It seems to me that you *do* need to join together. Each way of life is failing and if you don't do something about it, Emil…Yannis…,' she added, noting Xan's confusion, '…will have full control of you all. You can't let that happen. He was almost successful on at least three other worlds that

I know of – I know for sure that OPOL was behind the troubles there.'

She looked round at their shocked faces, noting the lack of surprise from Ariadne, and continued. 'I don't know *why* he wants to control you, but he is working for a woman called Agathe. And she is power crazy, from what I've been told. You can't let them win.'

Turning to the Wilder leader, Evie continued. 'Santos, your people should join the city. Technology isn't really a bad thing, it's simply another tool that reduces the hard work needed just to survive. You know full well how much effort it takes to live as a Wilder – wouldn't it be easier on you all if you had some help?'

Santos nodded slowly, not necessarily agreeing but acknowledging her point.

'Ariadne, the people of Hantaiken are *too* dependent on technology, they've forgotten what it's like to look after themselves, to even think for themselves. They need to talk to the Wilders and rediscover themselves, to become less reliant. I really don't think they can do that without the help of the Wilders; apart from a few children like Xan, they've forgotten how to use their own wits.'

Evie looked at Xan thoughtfully. 'You have a vital role to play, I'd say. You are already dissatisfied with your implant and being told what to do. But I really don't think you would enjoy the Wilder life. You've already proven that you're brave and resourceful – it must have taken a lot of intelligence and courage to disobey your implant. But a Wilder life is a completely different experience, incredibly hard work. A way of life that embraces both worlds would suit you better, and your friends.' She waved her arms at the other children who had escaped with them. 'Your father's influence could help change this world – driven by you, Ariadne and Santos.'

She stopped to watch the emotions playing across their faces. She was aware that she almost had them, but something still wasn't quite right. She thought hard.

'Yannis will need to be stopped though,' she said. 'You won't get anywhere if he is still in control. Do you know of anyone who might replace him?'

Ariadne closed her eyes, sighed, then stood up straight, head held high. 'I feared this time would come. I will stand for the council. I should have done it cycles ago, when they first asked me. But I enjoyed my freedom as a scout too much. I'm afraid I've been ignoring what has been going on.'

She frowned, and loosened the neck of her shirt. 'I could see the growing influence of Yannis. I know exactly what he's really like, yet I let him carry on regardless. It is time I made amends, I could have prevented this.'

Evie exhaled as a weight seemed to lift from her shoulders. She concentrated hard, and sensed that some of the quantum channels between Hantaiken and the Wilders were already aligning and growing stronger. It might take many cycles before the world was how it should be, but it was getting back on track – and she could go home! Somehow…

Her eyes were drawn once again to the midnight blue of

the pendant nestling at the base of Ariadne's throat.

'That is beautiful, where did you get it?'

'I was given it,' replied Ariadne, twirling a lock of hair absentmindedly. 'A very old friend of mine told me to take good care of it, as he was going away and might not return.'

Evie examined the necklace more closely. Running her finger softly across the dull grey metal, the accompanying tingle told her all she needed to know.

'Would you give it to me? I can feel that it belongs with the other things that my mother found. It is very important.'

Ariadne bit her lip uncertainly. 'He told me never to let it out of my sight,' she said at last. 'I can't go against his last words to me, I'm sorry Evie. If it is that important, then maybe our paths will cross again?'

Evie looked at her in dismay and opened her mouth to protest, then yawned suddenly, her body clamouring for attention. She needed food, she needed sleep…and she needed to relieve herself. She turned and asked a passing Wilder where to go, sensing it wasn't the right time to press Ariadne further. She excused herself, then made her way to the crevice in the wall, skipping past the great fire and its cauldron of aromatic stew, and avoiding gangs of Wilder and Hantaiken children as they raced around, lost in play.

As she approached, she wrinkled her nose. This was definitely the right place. Holding her breath, grateful that technology allowed them to have decent toilets at least, she walked behind the cleft of rock and stepped into complete darkness. Feeling her way along, wishing she had brought a torch from the fire, she tried to guess where the latrine was.

'One more step,' she thought to herself, 'One more, and then I'll turn back and get a light.' She edged forwards a little further, then cried out in alarm as her foot encountered empty space. Flailing her arms, she fell forward into the void.

Opening her eyes moments later, she realised she wasn't drowning in a smelly cesspit. She breathed thanks as she groped around and felt soft, yielding fabric above her head. There was no space to sit up, so instead she crawled towards to the light on her left.

She emerged from underneath her bed, dusty and exhausted, the ring clutched tightly in her hand. She lay back on the carpet and closed her eyes in relief.

I'm so glad to be back, she thought, feeling the tingle shiver through her as she grasped the ring. Rubbing her eyes tiredly, longing for some peace and quiet, she stood and wrapped it safely with the other items, then began to stuff them into her bag. After a moment, she paused. Emil was on her trail and there was no telling where the net would send her next. She really didn't want to leave her father's possessions behind, not when both her parents might have died for them.

Using one of Ellen's scarves, she wrapped the bundle securely around her body. Remembering the neural disruptor in her bag, Evie tucked it into her trouser pocket then went downstairs, bracing herself for whatever lay ahead.

...CONNECTING...

'I almost had her!' growled Emil, thumping his fists onto a lifoNET capsule in frustration.

'Do that again and I will chop them off,' stated Agathe mildly.

He grew pale, knowing she wasn't joking. 'I'll get her this time,' he promised. 'And that traitor Aaron. I know exactly where they're hiding now. Release me from my other duties so I can focus on hunting them down.'

Agathe raised an eyebrow. 'Evie has beaten you several times already. You are quite clearly incapable of doing this alone. I am coming with you.'

He stared at her, trying to hide his doubt. 'Are you strong enough to capture her?' he cautiously asked.

She covered the distance between them in two swift strides and pulled against his unresisting body until he was staring into her cold blue eyes. Her dry, powdery breath washed over him as she spoke.

'Physical strength is not the only way to have a hold over someone, my dear. I was hoping you would have learned that by now. Your body is stronger than mine, but I have control of you, and always will. You are weak, I am strong. I will capture Evie.'

She dropped her hand in disdain. 'I remember how to be maternal, Emil. Evie will lap it up,' she said confidently. 'Even I felt…well, *something* during the first flush of motherhood.'

Her mouth twisted at the astonishment on his face. 'Oh, don't worry, it didn't last long,' she assured him. Pain and sorrow darted so quickly across her face that he was sure he'd imagined it. 'After the baby was born, I swore no-one would ever control me again.' Her features hardened and she gestured to him impatiently.

'Come, we have much to do. Give me the coordinates and go. Don't do anything until I get there, don't hurt anyone, and let me do the talking. Do you understand?'

He nodded sullenly, his handsome face darkening at her tone. She stared at him warningly while he activated his el-VA, his fingers shaking under the scrutiny of her flinty gaze.

She didn't bother watch his molecules dissipate but instead smiled hungrily as she turned to Ellen's capsule. 'We'll have her soon,' she whispered quietly, exultantly, a smirk playing on her lips. 'And then what fun we'll have.'

With a final rap of her knuckles on the smooth surface, she activated her el-VA and followed Emil to Earth.

'Aaron? Aaron? Where are you?' called Evie as she trudged down the narrow staircase. 'Aaron, please – I need to talk to you!' Panic tinged her voice when he didn't answer.

She ran quickly through the old cottage, cold sweat making her shiver. *What if Emil has already been here, what if he's already dead?* Becoming increasingly frantic after every empty room, she suddenly stopped and sniffed. Slowly, she opened the kitchen door to find Aaron flapping at the burning toaster with a tea towel, trying to quench the flames as they slowly melted the plastic casing.

'Don't just stand there, help!' cried Aaron, noticing her in the doorway. 'Didn't you hear me call you ages ago to look after the toast?'

Evie shook her head in amazement. 'No, I've been rather busy as a matter of fact. I couldn't hear you from where I was.'

Pushing him aside, she picked up a wooden spoon to turn the plug off at the wall. Grabbing the towel from Aaron's clutches, she soaked it in water, draped it over the toaster, and watched in satisfaction as the flames gave a final flicker and died under the blackened cloth.

'Honestly, you're a liability sometimes!' she scolded affectionately, shaking her head. Her heart tightened as she watched him standing there, head hung dejectedly. Without warning, she burst into tears and flung herself at him.

'Oh Aaron, I was so worried something had happened to you,' she sobbed, mucus running from her nose onto the soft wool of his jumper.

'Don't worry, it was only a toaster,' he replied, stroking her hair. 'And we're safe enough here. As long as *you* cook.'

'That's just it, I don't think we're safe anywhere,' cried Evie. 'I've just been to Hantaiken, where Ariadne stopped me from freezing to death, and the city people have implants and are being controlled, and the Wilders can't survive on their own. Oh, and Emil tracked my surge and captured me to take to Agathe. I only escaped because Ariadne helped me.'

Her breath hitched as the story tumbled out. Aaron squeezed her tightly while she wept, his expression turning thoughtful. He gently prised Evie's arms away from her body and looked into her eyes.

'Did you notice whether Ariadne wore a dark blue pendant, Evie? Please try and remember, this is very important.'

She eyed him in astonishment. 'How on earth could you know that?' she questioned, her quick mind working fast. 'She thought I reminded her of someone, but it can't be you as we're not related. How do *you* know who she is?'

He was quiet for a moment before replying. 'She is my sister, my twin in fact.'

Evie's mouth gaped. 'Your sister? How…what…?'

'We were sent away from our parents as babies. We never did find out who they were, or why they didn't want us.' He sat heavily onto a kitchen chair.

'I was sent to Edrioch, taught to fight from an early age. Ariadne was sent to Ukuthula, a place of learning. We had no idea each other existed until many years later, when I moved to Eigenstat to become an OPOL agent.'

He abruptly stood and began pacing the room, hands clasped behind his back.

'We'd had a security breach at lifoNET, someone had managed to access the mainframe. Emil rushed off, leaving his workstation unattended, and I just happened to take a look.'

'You were being nosy, you mean,' said Evie, laughing a little.

'Well, I must admit I was curious. Especially when I saw my name across one of the documents. That's when I discovered I wasn't an only child after all, but had a twin sister. By then, she was living on Hantaiken. I would have read more, but Emil came running back and I knew he wouldn't appreciate me prying. It was only later that I thought to wonder why he had access to my personal information.'

He stood for a moment, lost in memories.

'I travelled to Hantaiken with my el-VA, of course. I had to meet her. Luckily, she was as glad to see me. We've kept in touch ever since.'

He stopped and looked intently at her.

'She had quite a lonely life on Ukuthula in those early years. It is basically a vast library, filled with nothing but books. She lived with your father there, you know,' he added casually. 'He gave her that pendant before he disappeared.'

Evie sank onto a chair, once again overwhelmed.

'Everything really is connected,' she whispered, her head spinning.

'Let me get this straight,' she said, concentrating hard. 'My parents were both agents of OPOL. They fell in love, had me, and my mother left the agency. My father carried on and stole some plans to destroy lifoNET, hid them, then disappeared. You were separated from your twin at birth, ended up becoming an OPOL agent, and worked closely with a psycho who is now trying to capture me.'

'He wasn't that bad then,' he protested. 'The signs were there, I guess…but he was my friend.'

Evie carried on, raising an eyebrow at his words. 'You were sent to spy on me and Mom after Dad vanished. You ended up falling in love with her, but she went missing. Then you left the agency to keep me safe. Thanks for that, by the way.'

She stood to grasp his hand, grateful for his presence.

'I find out I'm a naquant, travel to some really, really strange places, and your twin sister saves me from that psych…sorry, your former friend. Oh, and don't forget the mysterious Finn, who appears out of the blue just when I need him the most.'

She looked at him, incredulous. 'If this was a story, no-one would ever believe it, it's ridiculous.'

'The net works in mysterious ways,' smiled Aaron, his eyes twinkling.

Turning serious, he said, 'Evie, for whatever reason you are clearly a lynchpin – events are unfolding, with you at the centre. We don't seem to have any control over this, and have no idea what will happen next. You need to be prepared for anything.'

He squeezed her hand tightly.

'Trust your instincts at all times. You will know the right thing to do, at the right time. And you have to believe that the net will aid you, so that life can flow back to the right track. It isn't always like this, you know.'

'I hope not,' said Evie, fighting a yawn. 'I'm shattered already.'

Wearily, she stretched, but halted midway, shocked as a loud horn sounded outside. Aaron swung round in alarm.

'The tripwire, someone's out there,' he warned. 'Quick, we don't have much time.'

Grabbing her by the arm, he dragged her over to the cellar door.

'The lonely location wasn't the only reason I chose this house,' he explained, grabbing a torch from the top of the cellar and handing it to her, before urging her down the steep wooden stairs. Quietly, he bolted the door behind him and followed, steadying her as she stumbled into the cold room carved into the cliff below.

'Over there,' he whispered loudly, gesturing to the corner. 'We need to move those boxes, and quickly. There is a passageway that leads down to the beach. We need to get to the boat before Emil catches us.'

'How do you know it's him,' she asked, skin crawling as she heaved an old wooden crate thickly covered in spiderwebs.

'I don't, but I'm not taking any chances. We know he can track you, so he probably followed you back from Hantaiken. I won't let him get you.'

He cursed as he dropped the last crate in his haste. The loud crash echoed around the small chamber and he winced as he looked at Evie. Working quickly, he kicked the broken slats away and fit a key into trapdoor beneath. Straining as he lifted the heavy wood, he ordered her down the crude stone steps.

'Be careful,' he cautioned. 'It's a bit slippery down there.'

Condensation oozed across the dank stone walls, making Evie shiver as she carefully eased herself down. Aaron followed and lowered the trapdoor behind him. A loud splintering at the cellar door made him lose his grip on his keys as he tried to lock it from below. Knowing time was short, he abandoned his attempts and slid home the bolt instead, hoping it would hold. Taking a breath to steady his nerves, he followed the light from Evie's torch as it bobbed ever deeper into the cliff.

Emil growled in frustration at the bolted trapdoor, then raced back up the stairs, pushing aside the remains of the cellar door.

'I can't open the trapdoor, I need a crowbar or something. Help me look, they're going to escape,' he shouted to Agathe, who stood there unperturbed.

She sneered at him. 'Clearly there is a passage down to

the beach, where there is no doubt a boat waiting. Instead of flapping around, I suggest we go and see if there is another way down.'

She flicked her hands dismissively, causing him to flinch. He slunk out of the house and began searching the cliff edge.

'Here!' he called, the wind whipping his words away. 'I've found it.'

She motioned him out of the way and nimbly climbed down the sheer track. He followed, careful not to dislodge any stones onto her dazzling white hair. *Just one little push, that's all it would take,* he thought as he watched her navigate the fragmented trail. *I could be free again.* He clenched his fists as he fought temptation, then froze when she suddenly stopped and turned to stare. A chill swept over him as a knowing smile flit across her lips, before curling in contempt. Deliberately turning her back, she continued down the narrow path. Emil followed silently, sweat dried by sudden terror.

Reaching the end of the passageway, Evie gasped as her face was blasted by saltwater spray from white-tipped waves crashing over the stony beach. Strong winds tore at her, and she crouched behind a large rock for protection while she waited for Aaron. She could see a small boat pulled high onto the sand and hoped he knew how to row. Glancing up, she cried out at the sight of two figures making their way carefully down the cliff, the hulking frame of one all too familiar.

'He's here,' she whimpered to Aaron, who squatted next to her. 'And he's not alone.'

He peered up at the cliff face, blanching when he saw the old woman.

'Agathe,' he murmured, his mind furiously planning their chances of escape. 'We need to get to that boat.'

'But they're almost at the bottom, we won't reach it in time,' cried Evie, fear cracking her voice.

'Did you bring your disruptor?' he demanded, thinking fast.

Evie fumbled it out of her pocket and handed it to him.

'You keep it,' he said, after setting it maximum stun. 'Try and get Emil, he's the immediate danger. Although certainly not the most dangerous. The range isn't great, so you'll need to get closer. But not close enough for him to grab you. I'll deal with Agathe. Quick, go!'

He ran across the sand, staying low, and called out to distract from Evie, who was scurrying from rock to rock, edging ever nearer to Emil.

'Agathe, stop. I won't let you take Evie, you know that. This madness has to end.'

Agathe braced herself against the wind and looked at him, amused.

'I don't think so, dear Aaron. I need Evie, and I mean to have her.'

She took a few steps away from the cliff as Emil reached the bottom and aimed his own disruptor at Aaron.

'No need for that,' she said, pulling his arm down. 'Evie

will come quietly when she hears what I have to say.'

'No, I won't!' shouted Evie furiously, as she stood up from the shelter of a rock. 'I don't know why you want me, but I do know you killed my parents. I will never go with you, ever!'

She aimed the disruptor at Emil and activated it, her hands shaking. Her heart sank as she realised it was still on narrow beam and she missed. She fired wildly again, and Emil ducked to avoid the dazzling blue light. His scowl deepened and he crouched, ready to spring. A light touch on his shoulder held him back, and he warily watched as Agathe coolly walked towards Evie, a gentle smile on her face.

'You don't need to fear me, my child. I would never hurt you. I need your help, that is all.'

She took a step closer, eyes wide and imploring. Evie looked at her, confused.

'But you took my parents from me,' she said, the disruptor wavering as she tried to keep it steady.

'They knew my mission was important,' explained Agathe, holding out her hands. 'Both of them have helped me so much.'

She took a step closer to Evie, who began to lower her trembling arms.

'I can take you to see your mother, you know. She has been missing you.'

Fierce joy pierced Evie's heart. 'She's alive?' she whispered, not knowing whether she could trust this delicate, kindly woman.

'Yes, of course. She is still full of energy. Take my hand and we can go and see her. I will show you exactly what she's being doing for me these last few years.'

Evie stifled a sob, uncertain, as Aaron called out to her.

'Evie, no! Don't trust her, she usually lies. Even if your parents are alive, I doubt they are working for her willingly. They would have never left you alone.'

He moved closer towards her as she stood biting her lip, torn between them both.

'But I have to make sure, Aaron. You understand that? I can't leave without seeing my mom.'

She began to take a step towards Agathe, then stopped as her vision wavered.

'Oh no, not now,' she breathed, as strands of the net coalesced before her eyes. Knowing she was unable to prevent it, she leaped towards Aaron instead and grabbed him tightly. Agathe could only screech in fury as they both disappeared before her. Hearing movement behind her, she whirled and clawed Emil across the face, leaving rivulets of blood trickling down his face.

She stood there for a moment, panting, forcing the rage deep down inside to where it had always prowled, ready to strike. Regaining control, her face an icy mask of calm, she took out her el-VA.

'I want the power in that girl,' she hissed, raising her eyes at the distorted double reading. As she watched, the surge split and headed towards two separate locations. 'No-one has ever been able to take a non-naquant with them, she is unique. And I want her.'

She turned to Emil, who was slowly wiping the drying blood from his cheek, shocked at her loss of control.

'These are the coordinates,' she said, transferring the data to his el-VA. 'One of them is Evie, the other is Aaron – it seems they separated mid-transfer. Do *not* hurt whoever you find, do you hear me? I want them both alive. You will follow this trace, I will take the other.'

She looked at him, exhilarated. 'Evie is the final step, Emil. Once we have her, nothing can stop me.' She turned to walk away, then stopped and thrust her face close to his. 'Do not mess this up,' she warned, dragging a fingernail across his eyelid before activating her el-VA.

Emil swept a hand through his hair, raggedly breathing the tangy, salty air for a long second or two, then translocated to the other location.

Deborah Nock

5. KNOWLEDGE IS POWER

'Librarians are the secret masters of the world.'

—*Spider Robinson*

Evie sat up, groaning, squinting at the brightness surrounding her. White lights pulsed across her vision, in perfect symphony with her throbbing headache. She hung her head between her knees, trying not to be sick, then looked around in alarm, wincing at the sudden movement.

Where is he? she thought frantically, remembering her tight grip around Aaron before the net took them away. *Please don't tell me I lost him!* Gulping back tears, his advice to trust her instincts and believe in the net echoed in her mind. She took a deep, steadying breath, then extended her awareness, worry making it hard to visualise the network. Finally it sprang into focus. Relieved, she saw that the channel connecting her to him was glowing and strong, although the node was distantly faint.

I'm sure he'll be fine, she reassured herself uncertainly, then became dizzy as a sudden realisation washed over her. If Agathe was telling the truth, and her mother really *was* still alive, she might be able to sense her as well. Concentrating hard, fingernails digging into her palms, she saw the connection to her mother stretching dimly away. Tears began to flow as she hopefully traced the strand. Her heart sank when she couldn't see the node at the other end, the channel ending abruptly, sliced clean.

She chewed on her lips in frustration, not knowing whether this meant her mother was dead after all, or something else. Head aching, she reluctantly accepted that she could do nothing else for the moment and decided to explore instead.

Evie clambered to her feet, eyes squeezed tight against the pain. She blinked, trying to focus, then gaped at the sight before her. She was standing on a balcony above a massive white room, cold, clinical lights banishing all shadows. Towering shelves stretched away into the distance, each filled with books, a dizzying riot of colour. But as she looked more closely, she realised they couldn't be normal books. She could see the cover of each, but the shelves themselves were wafer thin. She climbed down the nearby ladder to get a closer look.

As she approached, she noticed a slight shimmer over every book. Curiously, she touched the nearest one and gave a small squeak when the book flashed into life and words projected into the room. She began to read out loud.

'The hopes and fears of a nation were abruptly curtailed by...' Her voice faded as a quiet swooshing grew louder behind her. Turning, she saw a floating armchair flying towards her. She stepped back in alarm, then jumped as a soft voice gently enquired, 'Would you like to sit and read?'

'Err, no thanks,' Evie said. 'I was just curious.'

'Very well,' replied the chair, before floating a short distance away and hovering, clearly awaiting further instructions. She stared in amazement, tempted by the lure of the large, cosy-looking cushions, before turning back to the book and touching it again to close it.

'Just WHAT do you think you are doing?' boomed a voice. 'This is *my* Library, you are NOT allowed in here. Get out, don't you dare touch my books.'

She watched apprehensively as a tall, thin man stomped down the corridors towards her, face black with anger. Moving quickly, he grabbed her arms as he drew near, fingers pressing deep into her flesh.

'Get off me, you bully,' she shouted, trying to break free.

'Be quiet,' he said, giving her a rattling shake. 'I can only imagine you've come from that upstart's Library. The idiot is always letting people in to read and meddle with his books. You're coming with me right now.'

Giving her no time to respond, he dragged her along to a large door set in an alcove. As they walked closer, a beam projected from a device set high in the ceiling and scanned them both.

'Domain Master Tellis, verified. Young child, gender

female, human/uthilian hybrid, illegal entry into Ukuthula domain 6726,' intoned a voice from hidden speakers.

'Yes, I know that, you stupid computer,' snapped Tellis, impatiently. 'Open the door now so I can throw this creature out.'

'I'm not a creature, I'm a girl,' yelled Evie. 'And your computer really *is* stupid. I'm all human, not a hybrid.'

He ignored her as he dragged her to the door that had slid open. Beyond lay yet more stacks, this time lit by a gentle warm glow, soft and inviting. She could hear faint music drifting across the vast room and frowned, the simple melody itching at her mind. *I know that tune, where have I heard it before?* she wondered, before he threw her across the threshold and on to the carpeted floor.

'Get out, and stay out,' he ordered. 'Or I will have you sent to the mines without reprieve.'

He slammed his hand against the door control, and she watched him stalk away as the door closed silently behind him.

Wearily, she climbed to her feet yet again and sighed. Having no better options, she decided to follow the music. *Surely no-one who plays like that can be too bad?* She trudged off down the nearest corridor of shelves, turning at the crossroads whenever the notes began to fade.

It wasn't until she was becoming footsore and irritable that the music became loud enough to be heard just beyond the next stack. Taking a deep breath to steady herself against yet another unpleasant encounter, she stepped around the corner to say hello.

She watched him stand there, swaying, eyes closed, lost in the melody. His arms moved in rhythm to the mellow notes he was creating on a strange instrument. His fingers strummed what looked like lasers suspended between the floor and the contraption strapped to his head. A wistful smile hovered on his lips as he played, turning to sadness as the song finally came to an end. He exhaled along with the last notes lingering in the air, then opened his eyes. As his gaze fell on the figure standing in front of him, the blood drained from his face.

'Ellen!' he exclaimed, before falling to the floor in a dead faint.

Evie stared at him, shocked to hear her mother's name. Rushing to his side, she bent down and lifted his head, smoothing back grey hair still streaked with blond. Gently, she patted his lined cheeks to bring him round.

As she did, a memory clicked into place. When she was very small, her father used to play her a goodnight song before bed, which never failed to send her deeply asleep, wrapped in the knowledge that her parents loved her. After he died, her mother refused to play it and Evie's nights felt colder and bleaker. She had never heard it again…until now.

Looking down at the face in her lap, a choking sob escaped her as she finally recognised who he was. Her father. Her dead father. With a shaking hand, she scrubbed at the tears streaming down her face, unable to believe what she was seeing.

The man groaned to find a tear-stained, hauntingly familiar face looking back. He sat up and tentatively reached out to touch her face.

'Not Ellen. No, of course not. But how can it be? How can my little girl be here, right now? Are my eyes playing tricks on me, am I as mad as they tell me I am? Are you real? Evie, is that you?'

Evie wailed loudly as she threw herself into her father's outstretched arms. Her cries matched his as they clung to each other, hugging fiercely, not wanting to let go. An armchair hovered nearby, its neural network struggling to cope with the onslaught of emotion. 'Would you like to…sit down?' it asked tentatively?

'They told me you were dead,' Evie wept, half-laughing as the chair broke the tension. '

'I almost *did* die,' said Liam, stroking her hair, still not quite believing she was here. 'Agathe caught me, trapped me in one of her pods. I was on the brink of death, but had one last jump in me. And so here I am.'

'Pods, what pods?' asked Eve, sinking deeper into her

father's embrace.

He looked at her, considering how much to tell her.

'Evie, how did you get here? I must know before I explain further.'

Sitting back a little, she began to relate her story, interrupted by frequent questions from Liam.

'The last thing I remember was holding on to Aaron before the net sent me here. I lost him though, Dad, he's not here!' she cried, the tears beginning to flow again.

He hugged her tight, then sat in silence for a while, trying to work it all out while struggling to suppress his crushing anger and jealously that Ellen had found someone else to share her life, someone who Evie also clearly adored.

'Don't worry, my love. No naquant has ever had the ability to travel with another person before, you must be incredibly strong.'

She looked up at him, uncertain, and he squeezed her hand reassuringly.

'If I know the net – and I do, Evie, I really do – then Aaron will have been translocated somewhere else, where he was needed the most.'

He hesitated, unwilling to tell her the rest and burden her further; then sighed, knowing he couldn't avoid it.

'It all began when the net took me to the future,' he said, eyes troubled. 'Normally that never happens because the future can change with every decision we make. But I was taken to one reality after another, and in every single one Agathe's desire for power had led to utter terror, misery and suffering. I knew she had to be stopped. So I stole the master plans for lifoNET, with the intention of destroying it. Somehow, she discovered what I'd done.'

He stood to take the musical contraption from his head.

'I thought I was so clever. Finding a way to stop lifoNET, then hiding the plans and leaving clues where to find them, just in case she captured me. But I underestimated her. She caught me unawares, using Emil to betray me – my best friend!'

'What? You were friends? But he's working for Agathe.'

'I know that now. But at the time, he was the closest person to me apart from Ellen. My sworn brother, in fact. I let my love and trust for him cloud my judgement as to what he'd become. And so Agathe captured me.'

He licked his lips. 'That wasn't the worst betrayal though.'

Crouching next to Evie, he took her hands and held them tight. She looked up at him, not sure she wanted to know.

'They began to question me. Well, I say question – torture, more like. I wouldn't tell them anything, of course, the stakes were far too high. I told her I'd rather die. So Agathe pulled out her trump card.'

He closed his eyes as he remembered, his wrinkled face filled with pain. 'She told me she was my mother,' he sighed. 'After I was born, she left to protect me from her numerous enemies. But now she wanted me to join her, so we could "rule the universe together".'

He slammed his fist onto the floor. 'I refused her, of course. I had to. I couldn't let that future happen. And so she put me in the pod. My own mother.' He turned away from her, fury tightening his thin shoulders.

Evie sat back in shock. 'She is my grandmother? I am actually related to someone like that?!'

'Yes,' whispered Liam. 'I am so sorry. I grew up with dreams that my mother would be someone gentle, and kind, and loving. But she is not that. She is most certainly not that.'

She touched his arm timidly. 'Dad, what exactly *is* a pod?'

He scrubbed at his face, trying to clear his mind. 'It is how she powers lifoNET, Evie. Each pod contains a naquant, and she drains their naquant power. When they are empty, she throws away the husk.'

Her face paled, horrified to the core. 'How did you escape? Is that why you look so old now?'

'Thanks for the boost,' he chuckled, ruffling her hair. 'But yes, that is why I look much older than I am. She had been draining me for a long time and I didn't have much energy left. Not that I knew it, of course, I wasn't awake.'

He stopped, thoughtful. 'Someone revived me, turned off the power to my pod. I thought I saw Emil leaving the room, but I was groggy and close to death, so it could have been wishful thinking. I knew I had one last burst of energy left to overcome the naquant lock holding me in place and travel somewhere safe. I wasn't sure where, I just trusted the net. It brought me here.'

He stood again and gestured to the book-lined chamber. 'This is where I grew up, on Ukuthula. As did Agathe – until she had me, at least. After the…incident that led to my birth, she gathered all the data she had already found in this library, then abandoned me to create lifoNET. I didn't even know she existed until I moved to Eigenstat to become an OPOL agent, and certainly had no idea that she was my mother until just before she put me in that pod.'

He wandered over to a shelf and activated a book. 'Only these beautiful books kept me company growing up. And Ariadne, of course, abandoned like me. The domain masters had no interest in looking after either of us, so we looked after each other. We were inseparable, until I decided to leave.'

A sudden thought made her shiver. 'Does that mean I'm only half human after all?'

Liam smiled. 'Yes. Half human from Ellen, half uthilian from me. Not a bad combination, I must say. I met your mother when we were both training for OPOL. Emil was our tutor, despite being only a couple of years older. Emil, Ellen and me, the terrible threesome. We had such happy times.'

His face darkened. 'That changed when we found out that Ellen was pregnant. My friendship with Emil was never quite the same after that. He loved her as well, you see, with all of his heart. And I took her from him. No wonder he hates me.' He hung his head, filled with guilt but also defiance because Ellen had chosen him.

She stood and hugged him tight, still marvelling that he was alive. Then realised something that made her step back.

'I can't feel a tingle, Dad. Even though you're a naquant.

When I touched Anya or Finn, I got shivers all over me and I could see the net. But there is nothing with you. I can see the connection between us now, but I can't feel it.'

He turned towards her, saddened. 'I have no naquant energy left, my dear. I can no longer travel the net. I am here until I die, unless I can find an el-VA.'

He braced himself before continuing. 'Evie, I have to tell you something and you must be brave. Can you do that?'

She nodded, eyes widening in dread.

'Your mother, my Ellen…I think Agathe was telling you the truth, she is still alive.' He shook his head as her face broke into a smile. 'No, it's really not good news, I'm afraid. I think she must have put Ellen into a pod as well, there is no way she would waste all that energy.'

'She is draining my mother?'

Evie stood for a moment, then whirled to kick the unsuspecting chair still hovering nearby.

'I have to rescue her!' she shouted angrily.

'Shush, come here. If you can rescue her, then you should try. But Evie, lifoNET *must* be destroyed, that comes first. Even if it means that your mom and all the other naquants still trapped will die in the process. You have to understand how important this is, *everything* is at stake. Ellen knew the danger and was willing to risk death. Look at me, Evie,' he demanded.

She moved further away, unwilling to hear more. Gently, he took her chin in his hands and turned her head towards him. 'I know this is hard, sweetheart. And I won't force you to do it. It is a choice you will have to make when the time comes. You will know what to do then. But I had to warn you.'

She stood there, exhausted. 'It's too much, Dad. I can't cope with it all. I can't bear the thought of her alone and trapped, getting older and older. And I certainly can't think about letting her die!'

'I know, my love, I know. Come, let's not think about it for a while. Let me show you around.'

He took her by the arm and led her away.

Evie watched listlessly as her father talked endlessly and showed her his books. Her mind whirled with recent events. Finally, overcome by fatigue, she collapsed into the chair that was still waiting nearby. Liam paused and looked at her tired face. A wave of remorse swept over him and he strode towards a machine in a nearby alcove. Pressing buttons, he returned with a steaming cup of hot chocolate and a plate of biscuits. Evie wolfed it all down, ravenous, sighing as the sugar rush revived her flagging energy.

'I'm sorry love, I get carried away sometimes. Despite my loneliness here as a child, I love this place. A whole world dedicated to learning! When I returned, I missed you and Ellen so much. Only these books have helped me to forget for a while.'

She smiled at him, loving the wonder his eyes. 'Have you learned anything interesting?' she teased, mischievously.

Then groaned as his face lit up and he launched into another lecture.

'Well, my latest project has been to find out how all of this started,' he declared, waving his arms around.'

'What, this library?'

'No…the universe!' She watched as he rubbed his hands, excitedly. 'From what I understand so far, black holes are life's…buds, I guess you could call them. The black hole draws in substance from all around, consuming matter and energy until it reaches a critical mass. Radiation is then released in response to quantum effects near its boundary. Previous theory suggested that this radiation reduces the mass and energy of the black hole until it disappears. However, from what I know of the net, I think something else happens.'

He paused for dramatic effect. 'I don't believe for a moment that the black hole just disappears. Oh, the radiation certainly causes the 'hole' to shrink. But instead, it closes off in our universe and the resulting 'bud' on the other side – in a different plane of existence – explodes into life as a new universe…the Big Bang! Imagine, millions of black holes in our universe forming new universes. And the same happening within each of those universes – all creating one giant multiverse, connected by the net!' He sat there happily, waiting for her to comment.

Evie looked at him, incredulous. 'So, the Big Bang was just a pimple bursting on the face of reality?' she asked, her eyes dancing with mirth.

He looked at her, crestfallen. 'Well, that's one way of putting it, I suppose,' he said, his shoulders slumping. 'But I still think the idea has merit,' he added quickly, his unquashable spirit rising.

He grinned at the laughter on her face, and his eyes softened. 'So like your mother,' he said gently, his eyes filling with tears at the years lost.

Evie's throat tightened, and she coughed, trying not to cry again. She looked around her for a way to change the subject.

'It's a big library, that's for sure. I bet you could get lost for days.'

'My domain is only a very small part of it, you wouldn't believe how massive it really is. It used to be a normal library, you know, with paper books and scrolls. But a fire destroyed a big part of it. All that knowledge, lost. After that, everything that remained was digitally converted.'

'If it's all digital, why on earth do you bother with these shelves?' Evie asked, confused. 'Why don't you just have one computer each and bring up a book when you want it?'

'Because part of the joy of reading is to physically browse through the books – to see them displayed on a shelf, and wonder at what worlds lie beneath the covers,' replied Liam. 'You can't really do that with a computer, you miss all the good ones! This way, we can have all the pleasure without the need for flammable paper.'

He went over to the monitor built into her chair.

'We control the displays on each shelf and choose which

range of books we would like to see. Countless uthilians have scoured the worlds, always adding more and more books to our massive collections. Although having lots of knowledge hasn't necessarily made us wise,' he added, grimacing.

'The Library spreads over most of this world now,' he continued. 'It was split into domains, to make it easier to administrate. Each domain is fiercely protected by its own Domain Master, and none of them want to share their knowledge. These chairs are linked to a specific domain; the books of other domains are strictly off limits. A ridiculous notion, if you ask me. We should be sharing our knowledge freely to whoever might want it, not hoarding it like misers!'

Evie frowned as he stood there, agitated.

'God knows I love this world. But it is far from perfect. Each of these stacks contain millions of books, and there is a multitude of stacks across the world. Such data requires huge memory banks. Quotrum, the substance we use as digital storage, is plentiful on Ukuthula…if you don't mind mining for it. So that is what you will find outside the domains, deep mines searching for more and more quotrum.'

He stopped, saddened. 'It is an easy life for a Domain Master. But it's a harsh and bleak one for the miners, often very dangerous. I have tried to do my best for those who serve my own domain. I have improved their living conditions, and allowed their children to use my Library so they can learn how to read and write. It's the very least I can do – but even these small acts are too much for the other Domain Masters. As ever, power corrupts – and that is true even in this place of learning. They want me out, and they want my books for themselves.'

'Dad, why did the net send me here? Was it just to see you again?' asked Evie, stretching wearily. She had slept for a few hours, curled up on the comfortable cushions while Liam watched over her, gently stroking her hair in wonder and misery at missing so much of her life.

'It's a good enough reason if so,' he smiled, kissing the top of her head. 'But I think it's more than that. I have been wondering for a while how I could get this to a naquant.'

He rummaged in his pocket and held out a beautifully engraved old pocket watch with an open clasp on the back. Evie took it, feeling a familiar tingle. Confused, she saw that the numbers on the intricate face weren't the expected one to twelve, but one to seventy-two. There was only one hand.

'What is it? Do you have a different way of telling the time here?'

'We do, but it's not a timepiece. It controls the other items I hid, once they have all been put together. This will provide the coordinates for the location of the master plans. But only to a naquant…only they will be able to control the Bloch device.'

'Why can't you just tell me where the plans are?' wondered Evie.

'Because I can't run the risk of Agathe catching you, or any other naquant still free. She will torture you for the information. This way, you should be ready to act immediately once all the items have been assembled. I have hidden them in worlds that Agathe has already meddled with – I know the net will send naquants to undo the damage. They should be able to sense where they are, as the objects have been attuned to the net.'

'We've already found some of them Dad,' said Evie excitedly. She undid the scarf still wrapped around her body and lay the objects carefully on the arm of the chair. Liam looked at her, chewing his lip, torn between keeping her safe and knowing she might be the only one to stop Agathe. Reluctantly, he began to show her how it worked.

'You put the ring on like this. Then slot the disk onto the top and attach the lenses. This part here, which looks like an eyepiece, is actually a net projector and is used to focus the device. And my watch slides onto the rod to control it. It also provides the power when it is fully wound. The only thing that is missing, which will lock it all into place, is the net magnifier.'

'The pendant!' exclaimed Evie. 'You gave it to Ariadne. The stone would fit perfectly just here,' she said, pointing to the larger ring that was still empty.

He smiled at her proudly. 'Once the pendant is in place, you will be able to activate the Bloch by putting the code into the watch'

'Code? What code? Why don't you just give it to me now?'

'You will need to ask Ariadne for it,' he stated firmly, folding the items back into the scarf and handing the bundle to her.

'You are already at risk, especially if Agathe realises you have these items. She will stop at nothing to get them, even if that means hurting you. Ariadne is the key. If you can find her again, she will help you. You must destroy lifoNET!'

Just then, the door into the next domain slid open and Tellis burst into the room, closely followed by several other men.

'There is he is! Look, I told you he'd be showing the girl everything. He isn't fit to be a Master. I demand he be detained immediately and investigated. Those miners of his have been spreading word about his acts of 'kindness', and *we* have been reaping the consequences. Threatening to strike unless they receive better treatment...how dare they!'

He stalked towards them, incensed.

'Dad, what do we do?' whispered Evie, standing up to face the oncoming men. As she did, a movement caught her eye and she gasped as a now-familiar figure loomed from the open doorway, his shadow stretching away from the harsh glare behind him.

'Emil,' she hissed, tightening her grip on her father's arm. He turned and locked gazes with the big man, a barrage of complex emotions passing between them. The contact was broken as the Domain Masters moved closer, spreading to try and outflank them.

Emil began to slink behind a shelf stack as Liam's trained instincts kicked in. Coolly whipping out a device similar to Evie's disruptor, he fired at the approaching Masters and they slumped to the ground, unconscious. He heard a groan and a thump as Emil was caught in the backwash.

'Time to go,' he said, pulling Evie towards him and running towards the far side of the room. Set into the rock wall was a solid metal door. He punched in a key code, hauled down a lever mounted to one side, and turned the wheel. The heavy door began to swing open, the well-oiled gears moving smoothly.

'In here,' he said, pushing Evie through the half-open door. Behind them, he could see Emil climbing groggily to his feet, shaking his head to clear it. Liam watched as he recovered quickly and scanned the room. Seeing them both framed within the door, Emil bellowed as he gave chase. Liam's eyes widened in alarm.

'Run!' he shouted, shoving her forwards. He hurried after her as she sprinted away, knowing he had no time to close the door. 'We'll go towards the mines, we should be able to hide there.'

They raced along the passageway, the rocky floor hampering their progress. Liam looked back to see Emil trying to squeeze his bulk through the narrow gap, his face red with exertion. He smirked, remembering the times during training when he'd taken advantage of his own smaller, lithe body to beat the superior strength of Emil.

Clenching his jaw, he suppressed the wave of sorrow at having to fight his old friend. Knowing that man was gone, Liam urged Evie to go faster.

She ran, her blood pumping and legs rapidly tiring. She was fed up of running, tired of being in danger, and heart-sick at the thought of what was yet to come. She began to slow down, her breath rasping harshly in the humid, smoky air. Coughing, she looked around her as the passage opened up into a small cave.

'What is this place?' she wondered, staring at the plumes of yellow smoke that belched between cracks in the steaming rock. Sweat began to roll down her face, leaving clean trails in the dirt.

'This is where the mines begin,' said Liam, encouraging her to keep walking. 'It's not particularly pleasant here, but it's idyllic compared to the quotrum rock face. I could only stand that for a few minutes before I thought I was going to pass out.'

He guided her along a narrow path that ran alongside a deep cleft. She shivered as she felt the heat billow upwards, the thick haze hovering over the opening making it difficult to see clearly.

'No-one should be forced to work in a place like this,' he told her as they cautiously inched along. 'Anyone who chooses to do so should be well paid and looked after by those of us who gain most from their work, that's what I think. And they should be able to share the knowledge we have obtained, not be kept in ignorance.'

He grabbed her arm as she stumbled towards the edge. Gripping her firmly, he continued. 'Your arrival here could be the catalyst we needed. I have wanted to change things for a long time, Evie, but had become too complacent. Now that I've attacked the other Domain Masters, I have no choice. We need a mutually beneficial system in this world, before it implodes. I know how we can achieve that.'

He looked back to see Emil emerge into the cave. 'But first, we need to get you and the Bloch device to safety. And I need to deal with Emil. We can't go much further this way, it will be very dangerous without protective clothing. You need to access the net and let it guide you. You must end lifoNET, Evie. Remember, Ariadne is the key – find her.'

He gazed at her, his eyes softening, then hugged her tight, smelling the soft scent of her hair. 'You're a naquant, my love. I am positive you'll come back to me one day.'

She looked at him, memorising every detail, noting the grim determination etched into his face. The truth was, she had felt the net begin to nibble at her consciousness as soon as Liam shot the Masters. She knew her task in this world was complete, but she didn't want to leave her father so soon or abandon him while he was in danger. But as he spoke, the pull of the net became too strong. She raised her hand to caress his face, and faded away.

Liam watched her go, his throat tightening. Reluctantly, he turned to face Emil.

'Hurry up,' he taunted. 'As slow as ever.'

'Even being in that pod wasn't enough to keep *you* out of trouble,' growled Emil, pushing his sweat-heavy hair away from his face. 'Life was never quiet with you around.'

He looked at Liam, grimacing at the grey hair and wrinkled face. 'Some justice, I suppose, for taking Ellen from me,' he said, gesturing towards him. 'Not that it did *her* any good. Your stubbornness stole the life from her as well. And I am going to make you pay.'

With that, Emil launched himself at Liam and used his momentum to shove him onto the stony floor. Rocks bruised Liam's back while Emil's fists punched at his face. Dazed, knowing he couldn't beat him in a fair fight, Liam grabbed a hot rock by the edge of the crevice. Ignoring the searing pain, he pressed it into Emil's face, gagging at the smell of burned flesh.

Emil roared in agony and fell backwards, holding his hands to his face. Liam seized his chance and rolled away, then cursed as Emil's huge hand grabbed his ankle and dragged him closer. Flailing around, trying to free himself, Liam noticed a craggy spike of rock jutting from above. Frantically, his leg going numb from Emil's vice-like grasp, he fumbled the gun out of his pocket and fired. With a resounding crack, the spike broke away from the ceiling and fell. The sound of the tip spearing Emil's thigh was one Liam would never forget, nor the sight of the shock and pain in his friend's eyes before he passed out.

'I'm sorry,' choked Liam. 'I had to do it.' He stood over Emil and pulled on the spike, wincing when a spout of blood gushed out. Quickly, he took off his shirt and ripped it in half, tying it tightly around Emil's thigh to stop the bleeding.

The other half was used to compress the wound, until only a trickle of blood remained. After checking his pulse, Liam stood, satisfied that Emil would survive. Knowing he didn't have much time, he ran and disappeared into a maze of twisty, ever-descending walkways.

Agathe drummed her fingers on lifoNET's central console, eyes narrowed in concentration as she scanned the net display. Without sparing a glance at the pods surrounding her, she boosted the power to find Evie. After leaving Emil, she had followed the surge to Eigenstat, eager to finally harness the girl's potential – only to discover that her prey had already translocated, destination unknown. A missing el-VA made her suspect Aaron, few people knew how to cover their tracks so effectively.

The other surge had gone to Ukuthula. Agathe's eyes darkened as she remembered her childhood home, old hatreds distorting her face. She would raze the place to the ground if Evie was there. Frustrated, she sat back, unable to find any naquant activity on the world.

'Where are you,' she breathed, gripping the edge of the console. 'You can't have learned how to shield your energy already, surely?'

Abruptly, she stood and left the room, heading towards her quarters to wait for news from Emil. Her face hardened. *He* was becoming something of a liability, sentimentality was dulling his edge. She would have to replace him soon, before his usefulness was exhausted. Her lips curled in anticipation as she lingered on ways to rid herself of him. As she walked away, attention pleasantly diverted, she failed to see the surge on the screen behind her, a translocation from Ukuthula to Hantaiken.

...CONNECTING...

E mil limped through the mine, struggling to breathe the polluted air, sweat burning as it dripped onto his burned face. His thigh throbbed and he cursed Liam yet again as he pressed a hand to the crude bandage covering the torn flesh. Wearily, he stopped and leaned against the warm rock, wondering what to do next. His el-VA was damaged, broken in the fight with Liam, and he was lost in the dangerous tunnels. He could wander for weeks and never be found. Assuming that to descend was to die, he had been following the passages upwards but still hadn't reached the surface.

With a sigh, he pushed himself upright and trudged off, wondering where Agathe was. Distracted, he was almost at the end of the tunnel before he smelled the sweetness of fresh air. He sped up, eager to escape, then cried out in horror as his feet slipped on the loose gravel beneath him and out into open space. Frantically, he threw himself backwards as he began to fall over the sheer drop. His thigh banged against sharp rocks and he yelled in pain, grimacing as he felt warm blood begin to drip down his leg. He clutched at the stones, his fingertips shredding on the jagged edges, and dug in his toes. Gasping, arms straining, he held himself very still, not daring to move.

Cautiously, he glanced down and shuddered to see how high he was. A fall would kill him for sure. For a fleeting moment he thought about letting go, the urge to be free washing over him. Instead, he threw his arm up as far as it would go and scrabbled around to find a handhold.

'What the…' he shouted, as small hands wrapped around his hairy forearm and pulled, the muscles in thin, wiry arms bunching with the effort. He looked up to see a shock of silver hair peeking over the edge, then seized the chance to pull himself to safety. Trembling in exertion, he could only lie in shock and relief as Finn sat next to him, breathing heavily.

'It seems you needed a bit of help,' said Finn, patting his shoulder awkwardly.

Emil gave an explosive laugh and turned to lie on his back.

'Thank you,' he said quietly, giving him a look that went beyond thanks. 'I know I don't deserve your help.'

'You're right, you don't,' said Finn, offhandedly. 'But I couldn't let anyone die if I could do something to save them, not even you. I guess life isn't done with you yet, despite everything.'

He rummaged in his pocket and handed him the el-VA he'd stolen.

'I expect you'll be needing this,' he said, and stood. A sad smile crossed his lips as he stared down at the large man, wincing slightly at the burned flesh.

'Bye Dad,' he whispered, before disappearing.

Emil lingered for a while after he'd gone, heart heavy, summoning the strength to move. As he lay there, a thoughtful expression settled on his face. Reaching a decision, he stood.

'Enough,' he declared softly. 'Time to end this.'

Determined, he set the device to Eigenstat and home.

'Evie, wake up,' said a voice softly, hands patting her cheeks. She opened her eyes and looked around in confusion, then amazement as Xan's face stared back at her.

'Xan!' she exclaimed, pulling him closer to hug him. 'Am I really back on Hantaiken? Where is Ariadne, tell me, quick?' she demanded, rising to her feet and looking around the same cave she had left only a day or two earlier.

'Over there,' he said, blushing at the contact. He pointed towards the cave entrance, where two tall figures stood next to a burly man. 'With her brother, apparently, and Santos.'

Evie squealed in joy and raced over to them, Xan trailing behind. 'Aaron, I'm here!' she shouted, their faces turning to her in astonishment. Breaking into a wide grin, Aaron swept her up and swung her around.

'Oh, my dear. I was so worried about you,' he said, voice muffled as he pressed his face into her hair. He clung to her for a moment, before letting go and standing back a little. She turned to Ariadne.

'So, you couldn't keep away,' said Ariadne wryly, squeezing her tightly. 'And you are Liam's daughter! No wonder I thought I recognised you.' She held her at arm's length, studying her face. 'You look so much like him,' she said, sadly.

'I know!' replied Evie, excitedly. 'I've just been with him, he's still alive, he really is.'

She laughed at their shocked faces, noting the similarity between the twins as they stood together. While Santos gave her a quick bear hug, she told them what had happened on Ukuthula, watching Ariadne's face light up and the tears fall at hearing her beloved Liam had returned to their childhood home, while a shadow crossed behind Aaron's eyes.

'I had to leave him with Emil though,' said Evie, lips narrowing as she tried not to cry.

'I wouldn't be too concerned. He once told me he could always beat Emil, eventually,' said Ariadne. 'I'm sure he'll be fine. Besides, there is nothing we can do, so there is no point worrying.'

Sniffling, Evie licked her suddenly dry lips, unsure how to tell them the worst part.

'Dad also told me that Mom might still be alive, trapped by Agathe in one of those horrible pods, the energy being sucked out of her.'

Aaron grew still and pale. 'Are you sure?' he asked.

'No, not really. But it would explain the dreams I've been having. And I've discovered I can sense the link between us, although not her node. Oh, Aaron, what are we going to do? And that's not even the end of it.'

She hesitated, feeling almost ashamed at what she was going to say next. 'Please don't hate me…but it seems Agathe is my grandmother. She told Dad the truth, just before she imprisoned him in the pod. How could she do that to her own son? I am not like her at all, really I'm not!' she declared hotly, feeling her cheeks burn as they stared at her.

'We know, dear heart, we know,' said Aaron reassuringly, locking eyes with Ariadne and raising an eyebrow as he hugged Evie.

'How did you get here, anyway?' she asked suddenly. 'I thought I had lost you in the net.'

'I remember you grabbing me on the beach,' replied Aaron. 'The next thing I knew I was waking up on Eigenstat with a thumping headache. I didn't want to run the risk of bumping into Agathe if she came back to use lifoNET to track us, so I grabbed the nearest el-VA, tweaked the transponder so it wouldn't leave a trace, and came here to find Ariadne. We were just discussing what to do next.'

'Dad told me we have to destroy lifoNET. He's seen what the future will be like if we don't stop Agathe. He wouldn't tell me what happens, but I could see how much it scared him.'

She began to unwrap the Bloch device. 'These all fit

together and will tell us the coordinates for the master plans. But first we need the pendant he gave to Ariadne to complete it. Once everything is locked into place, he said Ariadne has the key to operate it.'

'Key, what key?' wondered Ariadne. 'He didn't give me anything but this.' She released the dark blue stone from the grey filigree and handed it to her.

'Here goes,' said Evie, slotting the stone into place and winding the pocket watch. Everyone looked at the device, expectantly.

'Well…that was rather underwhelming,' Evie remarked, turning the device over to inspect it. 'I was expecting *something* to happen, even without the key. I can feel that it's complete now, there is energy trapped within. Just waiting to be released, I guess. Any ideas?'

'What does the watch do?' asked Aaron, gently taking the Bloch from her.

'Dad said it controls the device and provides the power. But he wouldn't tell me what the key was, only that Ariadne had it.'

'But I really don't have anything else,' said Ariadne, becoming annoyed.

Evie stared at her, frustrated.

Aaron carefully inspected the Bloch. 'There is only one watch hand, how unusual. And why do the numbers go up to 72, it must signify something?' He looked up at Ariadne. 'Do these numbers mean anything to you?'

She blew out a breath and pursed her lips. 'I'm sorry, I

can't think of anything,' she said eventually.

'Hmm…there seems to be an engraving on the inside of the ring and on the disk, but I can't read it. Evie, you have young eyes, can you see what it says?'

She took the device and squinted at the miniscule text engraved into the grey metal. 'I think the ring says 'Hnabeyig'. And on the disk, the words say 'Unbbul Onobla'.' Confused, she looked up into Ariadne's startled face.

'But of course!' exclaimed Ariadne. 'Liam was always obsessed with dead languages and he taught me this one. We used it as our own secret code, even as adults.'

She smiled at them, jubilant. 'It means 'Birthday Little Sister'. So maybe we need to enter my birthdate?'

'Oh…Ariadne *is* the key, not *has* the key,' said Evie, remembering her father's exact words. 'Try it, see what happens.'

Ariadne licked her lips as Evie handed her the watch. 'Uthilians have a complex way of recording dates,' she said. 'I need to get this exactly right.'

'I was born on the second day,' she said, and tried to move the fine strip of metal clockwise to the second mark. She looked at the others in confusion. 'It won't budge.'

'Let me try,' said Evie, tutting. 'I'd forgotten only naquants can control it.'

She slid the ring onto her finger and took a deep breath. 'Here goes,' she said, and gently moved the hand to mark number two. As she did, she felt a shift in the energy. 'It's

175

working,' she said, eagerly. 'What's the next number?'

'Well, my full birthdate is the second day, which you've already entered, of the forty-ninth week, of the seventh month, of the twelfth rotation, around star QUA28-5, in galaxy QBT72.'

Evie continued moving the hand clockwise and anticlockwise, counting under her breath and feeling the net align as the hand reached the right marks. Biting her lip, she looked up apprehensively before moving the hand to the final mark. As it slid into position, Evie cried out at the surge of energy and stumbled, steadied by Xan who was hovering nearby. A sphere of dark blue light bloomed from the pendant, through the two smaller lenses, and blossomed outwards from the eyepiece. The sphere grew bigger and bigger until it surrounded them, filling the cave, blurry lights shimmering throughout its depth.

'Turn the eyepiece to focus it,' suggested Aaron, amazed at the glorious sight.

She twisted the sections, and the kaleidoscope of gentle glows jumped into pinpoint sharpness, glimmering clusters linked by sparkling strands.

'The net,' she whispered in awe. 'It looks just like the net.'

She turned around, trying to take it all in. 'But what does it mean?' she wondered. 'How do we find the coordinates?'

'Look, over there!' shouted Xan, his sharp eyes noticing a pulsating spark at the far end of the cave.

'I see it,' replied Aaron, walking towards it and peering up. 'And I *think* there's a number next to it,' he said. 'I need something to stand on so I can get a closer look.'

Santos strode over, motioning for one of his Wilders to follow, and they boosted him higher.

'Yes!' he called out. 'Definitely coordinates.' He groped in his pocket for his el-VA, entered the numbers, then signalled to be let down. He looked in astonishment at the location shown on the device.

'Surely not, why on earth did he hide them there?' he said irritably. 'I'm not sure whether he was being clever or stupidly cheeky. But according to these coordinates, Liam hid the plans…on Eigenstat! In the main control room for lifoNET.' He frowned at them in dismay, knowing the obstacles they would face if they decided to retrieve them.

'He probably hid them there so we'd have immediate access to lifoNET, to destroy it more quickly,' said Evie defensively, sensing that Aaron felt some hostility towards Liam. Fleetingly, she wondered whether he wasn't entirely happy to hear that her father was still alive. Dismissing the thought, she removed the Bloch from her finger, feeling a pang of loss as the wondrous display disappeared.

'I need to go there anyway. If there is any chance that Mom is being held against her will, I need to check it out. Are you with me?'

Aaron looked at the hand she held out. Gripping it tightly, he grinned fiercely at her. 'Of course I'm with you.'

'Count me in,' declared Ariadne, grasping their arms. 'You're going to need all the help you can get. Aaron, you can translocate me with your el-VA. Evie, do you think you can reach lifoNET alone?'

Evie closed her eyes, reaching out for the strand that might lead to her mother. 'I think so,' she said, hesitantly. 'Close enough to where she should be, at least – if she's still alive and it's not her grave after all,' she added, apprehensively.

Ariadne squeezed her arm. 'Let's get there first and worry about that later. Not only do we need to find the plans and Ellen – and release the other naquants, of course – we also need to work out how we're going to destroy lifoNET. Come, let us eat and sleep, and then start planning. We have a lot to do.'

She guided them through the cave towards the ever-present fire and the promise of food. Evie trudged along, torn between wanting immediate action and battling the tiredness that threatened to overwhelm her. Fatigue won, and she sank down in front of the fire. After eating a plate of the hot, rich stew handed to her, she rested her head in Ariadne's lap and quickly fell asleep.

6. LETTING GO

'Everything we do impacts on everything else.'

—Prof. Brian Cox

'Are we ready?' asked Evie nervously, looking intently at the calm faces surrounding her.

'As we'll ever be,' replied Aaron, giving her a reassuring wink. 'Is your communicator still working okay?'

She tested the small device pinned securely to her jumper, a small smile on her lips as she listened to her tinny voice being transmitted.

Aaron gave a thumbs up, then checked the coordinates on his el-VA. He put his arm around Ariadne and pulled her close. Evie closed her eyes, trying not to think of all that could go wrong, and searched for her link to Ellen. Alarmed, she sensed that it was fainter than before.

'We're running out of time, we must hurry,' she urged, looking worriedly at Aaron. 'Mom is getting weaker. Please don't let her die.'

Aaron nodded in understanding, and activated his el-VA. Evie watched them disappear, then took a deep breath. Xan could only stare as she gave him a tremulous smile and faded from view.

As consciousness returned, she became aware of a dry, metallic tang saturating the warm air, the quiet hum of cooling fans whispering across a vast chamber. Quietly, she stood and warily looked around for OPOL agents. Her mouth gaped in astonishment as she craned her neck at the enormous machine filling the room. Clusters of pods nestled around the central column, their harmonious whirring almost hypnotic. *lifoNET!* she thought, awed by the majestic machine. Sudden realisation made her spin around and she rubbed at the transparent cover of the nearest pod, frantically wiping away the fine condensation.

Her knees buckled when she saw the familiar face trapped within. She cried out in horror at the lines etched around the once lively eyes and silvering curls plastered to a wrinkled forehead. Sobbing, she sank to the floor, elation at finding Ellen mixed with grief at her stolen youth.

It was a long time before she could force herself to move again. Only the sharp metallic voices shouting in alarm through her communicator made her climb wearily to her feet. She turned away, unwilling to look too closely at her mother just yet.

Guiltily, she realised that Aaron and Ariadne weren't in the control room with her, and strode over to the door. Slamming her hand onto the control panel, she watched as the door slid open, then ducked as dazzling beams were fired towards her. Aaron half fell into the room, dragging his twin with him, her foot just clearing the door before it closed. He lay there panting, before raising himself on an elbow to look at Evie.

'Took your time, didn't you,' he remarked, eyebrow raised. 'Although how you managed to bypass the shield and translocate directly in here is a minor miracle.'

'I'm sorry, I really am,' she said, shamefaced. 'But, well...I found Mom. Oh Aaron, she looks ancient, an old woman!' The tears started to flow again as she stood there miserably.

'But she is alive?' he demanded, standing to hold her gently by the arms. She nodded, and dragged him over to the pod. Fearfully he peered down, gazing at the beloved face within. Then began to chuckle quietly, sniffing away his tears. Cupping Evie's face in his hands, he affectionately kissed the top of her head.

'Well, she might look like she's in her late forties now, but she's hardly ancient. Let's see how we can get her out of this thing.'

He examined the display next to the pod, frowning. 'We need a code,' he said, looking up at them. 'Maybe it's included in Liam's plans, he must have known we would need to release the naquants trapped here?'

Taking out his el-VA, he checked the coordinates that the Bloch device had revealed. Relieved, he saw that they covered only one small segment of the enormous room.

'Over there,' he said, pointing to an area behind the bank of el-VAs. 'That's where the plans should be hidden. Come on, we don't have any time to lose before more agents turn up. They can't get in here without Agathe or Emil, but I'm sure they won't be far behind.'

Ariadne squeezed Evie's hand, then ran to help Aaron search. Evie followed, staring uncertainly at the smooth walls and floor.

'Are you sure this is the right place?' she asked, doubtfully.

'There must be a hidden compartment built in somewhere,' replied Ariadne, confidently. 'Liam was always a technological wizard, he would have had no problem disguising it from prying eyes.'

But even she had to admit defeat after they had searched everywhere, using sensitive fingertips to reveal minute cracks in the unbroken surface. Sighing, they sat back on their heels and stared at each other in frustration.

'What are we missing?' wondered Ariadne, half to herself. 'Liam clearly wants us to find these plans, he would have made it obvious. Come on woman, think.' She tapped her forehead, vexed.

Evie sat, lost in thought. Suddenly, she leaped to her feet excitedly. 'We are such idiots,' she shouted. 'Only naquants can sense and operate the Bloch device, I am pretty sure only naquants would be able to find the hiding place.'

She grinned at them, then visualised the net, the process becoming more natural every time. As the network opened up, overlaying the flowing contours of the room, she laughed, delighted. Somehow, Liam had managed to leave a trace in the network, the large glowing arrow pointing to a spot a few feet below a light set flush into the wall. Around the tip of the arrow, ten random numbers shimmered on the smooth surface.

'It's here,' she said, still smiling as she walked up to the wall. Curious, they watched as she examined it, then shrugged, placing her fingers against the numbers in order and feeling a shift in the flow of energy. Their eyes widened as the metal seemingly *melted* to the sides to reveal a small opening. Inside was a flat parcel, securely bound. Eagerly, Aaron extracted it, removed the wrapping, and laid the document across his knees.

'Oh my goodness,' he whispered as he read the dense text. 'The man's a genius. Possibly mad…'

Falling silent, he examined the rest of the document, deep in concentration. He flinched violently when Ariadne poked him back to awareness.

'Well?' she asked. 'What do we do next, does it have the codes for the pods?'

He looked at them in dismay. 'No, there's nothing there. Only how we can destroy lifoNET.' He shook his head in wonder. 'Can you believe he's managed to find a way to trigger a mini black hole, deep in the heart of lifoNET's neural network?'

They stared at him, incredulous. He stood and began to pace. 'There is an incredibly powerful antimatter accelerator within the central column,' he explained. 'These instructions tell us exactly how it can be used to create the black hole. It will only remain stable long enough to suck the machine into it, most likely destroying it in the process. Then the hole will collapse…possibly explosively.'

He looked at them both. 'Liam says that he isn't sure how big the black hole will get. So as soon as it is triggered, we need to get out of here fast.'

'But what about Mom?' wailed Evie. 'And all the other naquants. We can't just leave them, to be flung into a new universe!'

'A new universe, you think?' said Aaron thoughtfully, his insatiable intellect distracted by the concept. Prompted by an irritated snort by Ariadne, he apologetically leafed through the pages, scanning the figures and diagrams to see if he could find any further information.

'I haven't got a clue,' he admitted, defeated.

'I have,' grated a deep voice from the other side of the el-VA stack.

They whirled round in fright, hearts beating fast at the unexpected intrusion. A harsh laugh broke from Emil as three pale faces stared him in shock. They recoiled to see his burn, the raw flesh oozing slightly at the edges.

'Oh don't worry, I'm not here for you,' he said, tiredly. 'If

Agathe wants you so badly, she can get you herself. I really don't care anymore.'

He turned towards Ellen's pod and stroked the surface. 'I am going to free her. It's my fault she's in there, and I've had to live with that decision every blasted day since. I'm going to be the one to let her out.'

Glancing at Aaron, he said, 'The code will open all the pods, I suppose you'd better release them as well.'

Rapidly, he entered the numbers on the keypad, his every move carefully scrutinised. There was a collective intake of breath as the lid rose slowly upwards, clouds of vapour billowing over the edge. Evie leaned over and gently touched her mother's lined cheeks.

'Mom,' she said, tenderly. 'Wake up, it's me, Evie.'

Ellen groaned as her eyelids began to flutter, then shot open in alarm. She struggled to sit up, flailing her arms.

'Get away from me!' she cried, seeing Emil hovering close, a strange look of dread on his face. 'I'll never let you harm my girl, ever! You stay away from her.'

She stopped, blood draining from her face when Aaron's face came into view.

'What…what's going on?' she asked, confused. She slowly turned her head to see Ariadne, and finally Evie standing there, helplessly crying.

Evie tried to swallow her tears as she gripped Ellen's hand, breath hitching. 'Mom, I'm here, I'm safe. Oh Mom, you've been gone so long, and I've missed you so much.' She rested her forehead against Ellen's arm, while her mother tentatively reached to stroke her hair.

'Evie? But you're all grown up, it can't be. I've only just been put in…here…' Her voice trailed off as flashbacks of terrible dreams pierced her mind, her skin shivering at memories of being trapped and helpless, and so very alone.

'How long?' she whispered. 'How long has it been?'

Aaron bent down to caress her face. 'It's been a few years, dear heart. But we thought we'd lost you, that Agathe had killed you.' He stopped and bowed his head, struggling to maintain his composure, the tears freely falling. Breathing deeply, he straightened.

'My beloved, I can't tell you how happy I am you're still alive, but we need to get you out of here and quickly.' He put his arm around her shoulder. 'Can you sit up?'

'Wait,' said Ellen, resting her hand on his arm. 'Just…wait a moment.'

She sat there motionless, probing the strange feeling of loss. Confusion turned to horror at the dreadful realisation she could no longer access the net.

'What have you done to me?' she grated, looking directly at Emil for the first time. Evie flinched at the pain in her voice.

He bent down and half reached towards her, imploring. 'Will you forgive me?' he asked quietly.

She looked at him, her eyes travelling across the once loved face. Reaching deep within herself, she sighed. Then slapped him with all the force her weakened body would allow.

'Never,' she spat, and turned her face away. Emil stood for a moment, his head hung low, cheek stinging, then slowly walked away.

'I'm sorry, but we must hurry,' said Ariadne, breaking the silence that followed. 'Ellen, I am so very glad you're alive, but we need to open all of these pods and get the naquants to safety before we destroy the machine.'

Ellen looked at her, wide-eyed. 'You found Liam's plans?'

'Yes, with Evie's help. She found him on Ukuthula, you know. He's still alive, but like you he's not a naquant anymore,' replied Ariadne, taking hold of Ellen's hand.

She winced as Ellen squeezed tightly at the news. 'He's alive, my Liam?' She fell back against the padded interior, overwhelmed. Then her eyes found Aaron's and a depth of sorrow passed between them.

'Oh Aaron, I have to go to him. You can understand that, can't you?'

He held her gaze, his heart shattering as she confirmed the worst fears he had buried deep inside after learning that Liam still lived. Knowing he had no time to mourn, he coughed to mask the hurt betrayal that was threatening to overflow. Licking his lips, he gave her one of his gentlest smiles.

'I understand, my love, I do. Go, with my blessing.' He bent down and lingeringly kissed her head. Abruptly, he turned and walked away, a tiny seed of resentment unfurling inside. Selecting an el-VA, he set the coordinates for Ukuthula and held it out for her.

'You'd better say your goodbyes,' he told Evie. 'She won't be coming home with us,' he added, trying to keep the bitterness out of his voice.

With one last, searching glance at Ellen, he walked to stand besides Emil, joining him in his misery.

'Mom? Why won't you stay with me?' asked Evie, distraught at parting so soon. Ellen grabbed her hands and hugged her close.

'My beautiful girl. I love you so much, don't ever forget that. But you need to get me out of here and I don't want to go back to Earth. I thought your dad had died in these horrible pods. I have to see him again. And I suspect he will know exactly what I am going through right now.'

She pushed Evie away slightly and looked into her eyes, marvelling at how much bigger she was. A solitary sob escaped her at the shared life taken from them.

'You have obviously discovered that you're a naquant,' she continued. 'You will be able to come and live us both once you have destroyed lifoNET. And you must do that, Evie. Agathe must be stopped. That is far more important than any of us, do you hear me?'

She looked into Evie's eyes and wiped away the tears. 'Can you be brave for a little while longer and finish what was started so long ago?'

Evie flung her arms around her mother and held her tight, realising the truth of her words. 'For you, anything,' she said, her voice muffled as her face pressed against her mother's neck. Eventually, she let her go and gestured towards the el-VA.

'Be careful on Ukuthula,' she warned. 'Dad was in some trouble when I left him.'

'He hasn't changed a bit, then,' replied Ellen, laughing slightly. 'I love you, dearest girl. And you Aaron, my darling. I am so sorry,' she continued, causing him to look back at her once more, grief twisting his face.

She gazed at them both, then took a deep breath. Straightening her back and looking straight ahead, she activated the device and disappeared.

'Well, that was emotional,' said Ariadne, dryly. Ever practical, she turned to Aaron who was still standing silently, watching the empty pod with troubled eyes.

'We need to open the other pods,' she said gently. 'Can you start the process to trigger the black hole, while we release the naquants?' She nodded, satisfied, as he inclined his head.

'Good. Emil, are you going to help us? Liam loved you, you know, and this would be the very least you could do to make amends to him and Ellen.'

Emil looked at her, drained, then rolled his eyes. 'May as well,' he grunted. 'Agathe is going to kill me anyway.'

He walked over to the nearest pod and punched in the number, waiting impatiently for the lid to open. Not trusting him, Evie warily followed at a distance, helping to revive the disoriented, tearful naquant within while he moved onto the next one. Ariadne scrambled to open the other pods, handing out el-VAs to anyone who had lost their ability to travel the net unaided.

Meanwhile, Aaron located the maintenance hatch on the central console and began entering commands into the inbuilt display, frowning as he struggled to follow the complex instructions. He had almost reached the end when a movement in front of him caught his eye.

'Need some help with that, dear boy?' drawled an amused voice. Aaron looked up, stiffening to see Agathe standing there, her disruptor pointing straight at him. His muscles tensed as he prepared to move.

'I wouldn't if I were you,' she warned, nonchalantly. 'This thing doesn't have a stun setting.'

She half turned to the rest of the room, frowning as Ariadne and Evie hurriedly sent the last naquant away.

'No matter,' she said sharply, not quite hiding her displeasure at losing her energy supply. 'There will be plenty of others to fill their places. Including you, little girl.' The predatory grin directed her way made Evie step back in alarm.

'But you're my grandmother,' said Evie quietly. 'Don't you feel anything towards me?'

'What, you mean *love* or something like that?' mocked Agathe. 'Don't flatter yourself. You have power, and I want it. And I will have it. I will kill everyone you love until I have it.'

Evie stared at her, sickened. She could see the certainty in her grandmother's face; nothing would stop her unless she surrendered herself. Knowing she couldn't let anyone suffer on her behalf, she blew out a breath. Before she could speak, her eyes caught a flash of silver hair heading towards Agathe, and her heart lifted.

'Okay, you can have me,' she declared, taking a step forward, head held high. 'I won't let you harm my family and friends any longer.'

An avid hunger gleamed in Agathe's eyes as Evie came another step closer, an exultant smirk playing on her lips. She held out a hand as Evie approached, then stiffened in surprise as a large figure emerged from behind the central console.

'You will need to get past me first,' said Emil, his disruptor trained directly on Agathe. 'I should have stopped you a long time ago.'

She looked at him in contempt, unsurprised by his betrayal. 'Yes, no doubt you should. But then, you were always weak,' she taunted, and shot him full in the chest.

'No!' shouted Finn as he threw himself at Agathe. They fell to the ground in a tangled heap, the old woman crying out in pain as the boy's solid body landed on her ankle, the sharp snap making Evie wince.

She quickly kicked away the fallen gun and turned to Emil. Horrified, she watched him slowly crumple into an open pod, bloodstains rapidly expanding across his wide chest.

Seeing her expression, Finn hastily extracted himself from

Agathe and limped over. His face twisted in grief as he gently held Emil's face in his hands.

'I can't be too late, I'm never too late,' he sobbed. With a trembling hand, he swept fine strands of blonde hair away from the older man's face. Emil opened his eyes and a radiant smile lit his face as he saw Finn.

'Son,' he managed to gasp, before his head fell back, lifeless.

Evie stared at Finn's back in shock. *I'm not the only one with a dodgy family,* she thought sadly, laying her hand on his shoulder in comfort. Aaron came and stood beside her, and sighed.

'It's time to end this, Evie. Before anyone else gets hurt.' Gently, he lifted the unresisting Finn away from Emil's body and closed the lid on his former friend.

'Come on, lad,' he said, passing Finn into Evie's care. 'Let's make sure his sacrifice isn't wasted.'

Quickly, one eye on Agathe who was writhing in pain, he walked back to the maintenance computer and entered a final code.

'Are we ready?' he asked, looking at them all. 'Don't forget, once I hit the send button, we need to get out of here.'

They nodded at him, eyes wide, and watched as he flicked a switch. Then looked at each other in confusion as nothing at all happened.

'That was a bit of an anti-climax,' said Aaron, scowling as

he looked down at the plans. 'Maybe I made a mistake in the programming?'

He studied the instructions closely, once again lost in awe at their complexity, until a small sound from Ariadne made him look up. He followed her gaze and gaped in astonishment.

The whole of the central console was *stretching* downwards, pulled by incredible forces. Evie opened her awareness and could see that even the net was being drawn inexorably down. Her eyes widened, and she took a step back.

'I think it's time to go,' she said, panic lacing her voice.

She dragged Finn towards the door, closely followed by Aaron and Ariadne. As Aaron thumped his fist on the door panel, she watched in terrified fascination as the rest of lifoNET disappeared, the powerful computer performing one last emergency protocol undetected by the humans fleeing the room. First one, then another pod was drawn into the widening hole, accompanied by an unearthly resonant warbling that made Evie's hair stand on end.

Beside her, Finn cried out as Emil's pod elongated and was sucked in. He closed his eyes for a moment, then whirled and hauled her through the open doorway. Behind them, the rest of the room continued to be pulled downwards, the black hole consuming the very fabric of the universe.

'Wait,' cried Evie, turning to see Agathe desperately trying to use her now defunct el-VA, unable to crawl to the door. 'We can't leave her. Not even Agathe deserves that.'

She moved towards what was left of lifoNET, but strong hands held her back.

'No,' shouted Aaron in her ear, struggling to be heard over the unnatural quaver radiating from the black hole. 'There's no time!'

She twisted as he pulled her away, watching her grandmother drag herself to a cupboard and press her fingers against a control panel. With the black hole growing ever bigger, Agathe pulled out an old, bulky device and calmly began entering a code. As the metal door slowly closed, warping slightly from the gravitational pull, Evie's final image was of Agathe's face contorting in agony as her leg was dragged into the gaping hole, before it finally snapped shut and her world exploded.

AND SO IT ENDS

The sound of a door creaking open drilled through Evie's awareness. Grimacing, she opened sticky eyes to peer around, blinking as her vision blurred. Her last memory was of a blinding flash and being forcefully thrown against the corridor wall. Then nothing, until she'd woken up, sore and bruised in this cool, white room, lying prone on a firm bed. A tube connected her arm to a fluid drip, and she stared at it in alarm.

'Where am I?' she croaked, struggling to sit up, her parched throat crying out for water.

'Hey, take it easy,' said a familiar voice. 'You're still on Eigenstat, in the hospital. You've been here for almost a week now! Your body is exhausted, you need to rest.'

Aaron limped over, hampered by the bandage around his knee, and slid his arm around her for support.

'What happened? Did we do it? Is IifoNET gone?' asked Evie, clutching at his hands.

'We think so,' he smiled, patting her shoulder. 'The

ceilings above collapsed when the control room was sucked into the black hole. There is nothing left but rubble, as far as our scans can tell.'

She looked at him, biting her lip. 'What about Agathe?'

'We found no signs of life. I'm sorry Evie, I know you didn't want her to die. But it's better this way, she can no longer cause any damage, and neither can Emil.'

She sat for a moment, melancholy washing over her.

'What happens now?' she asked, strangely deflated. So much had happened recently that she felt almost lost at having nothing to worry about or dangers to flee.

'We re-establish OPOL, of course,' replied Aaron. 'We will need the help of all surviving naquants, and we need to recruit more. Life goes on, you know. Naquants will still be needed to help civilisations, as you have done for millennia. I'm pretty sure you'll be busy for a long time.' He paused, his thoughts preoccupied by all that lay ahead.

'It's likely we could rebuild lifoNET,' he continued, standing to pace around the room. 'I have Liam's master plans, so it shouldn't be too difficult. Maybe in the right hands, it could do some good this time?'

Evie looked at him sceptically. 'I'm not sure anyone should have that kind of responsibility. The potential for misuse would always be too great.'

'Hmm…we'll see,' said Aaron, clearly not convinced. 'I know *I* wouldn't use it for my own benefit, at least. Anyway, we have lots to do before we need to worry about that.'

He stopped to gaze down at her. 'What are you going to

do, my dear, will you stay and help me?'

Evie looked at him, wide-eyed and stricken. 'Aaron, I love you, you know that. You're like a father to me. But Mom and Dad will be waiting. I just want to be with them for a while, be a normal family again. As much as we can be, of course, while fighting to overthrow the established order of a whole planet…'

She sniffed as a tear trickled down her face, tormented by guilt. Aaron watched her silently, conflicted. He knew she had to return to her parents. But a trickle of betrayal at being abandoned yet again twisted his heart, a small dark spot that threatened to spread. Shaking his head, he hugged her tightly.

'I understand, it is entirely your decision. I hope you will find time in the new world order to help me out though?' he asked teasingly.

She laughed, relieved. 'Of course I will. And Finn, I'm sure. Oh…Finn! Where is he? Aaron, I need to find him,' she said frantically.

'I'm over here,' grumbled a voice behind from a bed hidden by drawn curtains. 'I can't get any sleep with you two chattering away.'

Evie carefully scrambled out of bed and tottered towards him, dragging the fluid stand behind her. Aaron followed, steadying her when everything threatened to topple to the floor. She drew back the curtains and gasped to see Finn's face, glowing red from the blast.

'Ow,' she said. 'That must really hurt.'

'You tell me,' he replied, looking at her through swollen

eyes. 'You don't look much better yourself. We were lucky to get away so lightly though. I saw Agathe being pulled into the hole. It looked very painful. Serves her right!'

He coughed, overcome by anger and grief, and Evie gently took his hands. Once again, a pleasurable tingle ran through her body as their naquant energies entwined. She felt her awareness drift away, weaving into the beauty of the net. Vaguely, she heard a voice call her name, becoming ever more impatient. She snapped back to reality as Finn quickly dropped her hand onto the bed.

'Almost lost you for a moment,' he said, amused. 'Looks like I need to teach you a few lessons in how to be a naquant.'

She smiled at him shyly. 'I'd like that,' she replied softly.

'Ahem,' said Aaron, unwilling to intrude. 'I hate to break this up, but I must be going and you two need to rest. No more talking, sleep!' he ordered, escorting Evie back to bed.

Evie listened drowsily as he tucked her in, telling her that Ariadne had returned to Hantaiken to stand for council leader and undo the damage caused by Emil. In the other bed, Finn was already fast asleep and snoring slightly.

'That's good,' she said sleepily, eyes drooping. With a last warm look at Aaron, she began to drift off, safe and secure at last. Dreamily, she smiled at the thought of seeing her parents, the memory of all those books carrying her away.

Aaron smiled to see the two children, soundly asleep. Sighing at the buoyancy of youth, he squared his shoulders and left the room, mind swirling with the challenges he faced to resurrect OPOL. Lurking in the deepest recess of his soul, the potential power of lifoNETv2 began to fester. He would have been horrified to see gleeful anticipation twisting his lips into a smirk. Rubbing his hands, he set off to give his first orders of the day.

The beggar leaned casually against the wall, arms crossed as he watched the old woman make her way across the smooth concourse, ready to leap into action if her crutches began to slide. There was sometimes money to be made by being helpful, and pockets to pick if not. He looked with professional interest at the quality of her clothes and the fine linen bandages covering her knee, the lower leg missing. He might be able to eat all week after this little encounter.

Once again, he cursed his bad luck at losing his identity chit after a drunken brawl. He'd been struggling ever since to scrape enough credits to buy a new one, balancing that against the need to eat. He sighed, then twitched as the woman stopped to beckon him over. He pushed away from the wall, hesitating momentarily as he wondered why she was travelling alone through the seediest part of Serapis Station. Cold, calculating eyes swept over him as he approached.

'Take me to Zero,' she demanded, her voice low and hoarse.

'I don't know what you're talking about, lady,' he replied evasively, wondering how she could know of the shadowy hacker. That kind of information was dangerous, and his eyes glinted at the credit he could wring out of her. Suddenly, a seemingly frail hand clutched his throat and squeezed hard. He gave a strangled yelp.

'Do you want to see if you can call for help before I crush your windpipe? Take me to Zero, or I'll make you a eunuch.'

He tried to gulp as he looked down at the knife held close to his body. Glancing at her steely blue eyes, he nodded his consent then gasped as she released him and gestured for him to move. He scurried forward, thinking to lose her as she slowly followed on her crutches, but halted as she called out in a low voice.

'Don't think about running off, scum. I will hunt you down and make you regret it.'

He flinched at the violence in her voice, and resumed at a slower pace, careful not to get too far ahead. As she limped behind, occasionally grimacing in pain, he heard her muttering to herself.

'Not long now, girl, not long. Soon you'll be mine…and then you'll be sorry.'

THE END

(for now…)

GLOSSARY

Eigenstat – the world where lifoNET is based.

el-VA – a lifoNET virtual assistant. Agents of OPOL need to use one so they can access lifoNET and so travel the net.

lifoNET – the lifeforce network device, a quantum network supercomputer created by Agathe in her quest for power. LifoNET can create a quantum channel to any place or time and transfer a traveller's quantum state. But in contrast to the way naquants travel, the link to the original body does not have to stay open; lifoNET can instead create another link in another place and transfer the quantum state to new atoms there. In this way, lifoNET allows non-naquants to travel the net. It can also be used to identify key pivotal events that have happened within worlds. LifoNET can only be accessed at lifoNET headquarters by Agathe, or by agents using an el-VA.

Naquant – a natural quantum teleporter who has the inborn ability to transfer their quantum state across the net.

Naquants can observe the flow of the net and sense which direction in life is the most favourable. They try to guide pivotal people along that path, so that the majority of people can experience the greatest benefits. Naquants are sent to different places by the net itself, when it has been disrupted by outside forces.

Neural disruptor – a gun that uses a blast of energy to disrupt brain waves and so incapacitate a person. It can be set to a narrow or wide beam, depending on the circumstances.

OPOL – the Order for the Preservation of Life. For many generations, naquants were its sole agents, guided by the flow of the net. It is now controlled by Agathe and is made up only of her agents, who travel the net using lifoNET and an el-VA. OPOL is now dedicated to encouraging people to make choices that would disturb their world and send them into disarray, giving greater control to Agathe.

Quantum state – a factor that contains all the information about a person at a particular time and place, including their consciousness. Naquants, or agents using an el-VA, don't physically transport as such; only their quantum state or information is translocated along a quantum channel, from one set of atoms in their world to a new set of atoms in a different place or time.

Quantum Universal Network (the net) – the lifeforce that connects everything; made up of quantum channels that look like strands to naquants and joined by nodes (people and animals), as well as fainter connections between all other things, whether living or inanimate. It seems that life prefers a path of least resistance and certain events, if left to develop without interference, make the course of life run more smoothly. But sometimes obstacles get in the way, and even just one person's free choice might send a civilisation into a different, not necessarily beneficial direction.

Quotrum – the element that is used for digital memory storage, mined on Ukuthula.

A NOTE FROM THE AUTHOR

I am a freelance medical writer based in Norwich, UK. I have spent over 20 years writing about the body and various diseases, and wanted a change.

Connected is my first book. *Choices* is the second in the series, which will be released in 2021. In the meantime, you will be able to find out the real story behind certain fairy tales in *A Likely Story*.

If you enjoyed reading *Connected* (or even if you didn't…), would you be so kind as to leave a review on Amazon? Thank you so much!

Printed in Great Britain
by Amazon

59634084R00122